Cinnabar Summer

By the same author

When Summer Fades
Kingham's Folly

Cinnabar Summer

Danielle Shaw

ROBERT HALE · LONDON

Robert Hale Limited
Clerkenwell House
Clerkenwell Green
London EC1R 0HT

2 4 6 8 10 9 7 5 3 1

Typeset in 11½/16pt Palatino
by Derek Doyle & Associates, Shaw Heath
Printed in Great Britain by St Edmundsbury Press
Bury St Edmunds, Suffolk
Bound by Woolnough Bookbinding Limited

Dedicated to the memory of:

Mavis Edwina Bass

Geoffrey Stone

Bertie Whippy

Three very special people who enriched the lives of so many with their love, wisdom and laughter.

Chapter 1

Rosemary Fielding turned away from the kitchen window, her face tinged with sadness. Yesterday she'd prepared breakfast for three. Today it was just for herself and her daughter and tomorrow she would be all alone. Widowed for three years and at last rebuilding her life, she gave silent thanks for the many friends who'd helped along the way.

Ten minutes later, her earlier melancholy forgotten, she was feeling less kindly disposed towards her fellow men – or at least one in particular.

'You told him what? Oliver! You know I didn't say that at all. I merely said. . . .'

Pausing in an attempt to hide the hurt and indignation in her voice, particularly when the person at the other end of the phone was sounding so ebullient, Rosemary held the phone at arm's length. Seconds later she recalled exactly what she'd said when American impresario Oliver Duncan announced his intention to turn her debut novel into a mini-series and cast Stephen Walker in the leading role.

With a mumbled, 'Yes, I promise I'll be there,' she circled two dates on the kitchen wall-planner. On the first she wrote 'London – lunch with Oliver,' and on the second 'Rehearsals' followed by a row of seemingly endless exclamation marks.

Mildly curious, her daughter Jane looked up from where she was spreading marmalade on to her toast. 'What was all that about?'

'Oliver's invited me to lunch and, because I missed the earlier auditions, he's suggested I might like to attend the first day of filming.'

'Wow! Lucky you. So why all the gloom and despondency? I thought you couldn't wait to see *To Love the Hero* made into a mini-series. You're not upset because Oliver asked someone else to write the screenplay?'

Rosemary shook her head, still somewhat bemused by Oliver's concern regarding casting and auditions. She was also more than happy not to be involved with the screenplay. There at least she trusted Oliver's judgement.

'It's not Oliver I'm worried about,' she began. 'It's Stephen Walker. Oliver's insisted on signing him for the leading role.'

'Stephen Walker! Not *the* Stephen Walker who seemed always to be making tabloid headlines when I first started at uni? What's he done now?' Dropping her toast, Jane made a grab for the morning paper. 'He's not made front page news today, has he?'

'Thankfully not, as you can see for yourself,' Rosemary announced, peering over her daughter's shoulder at the day's shock-horror features. 'In fact, since the advent of all these boy bands and multi-million pound football transfers, Stephen Walker appears to be maintaining a very low profile.'

'Either that or else he's no longer tabloid fodder,' Jane replied, flicking hurriedly through the paper before returning to the front page.

'Tabloid fodder?'

'What Stephen Walker says and does is no longer of any interest. Despite his once-famous, rugged good looks and man-of-mystery persona, he has been looking a little bit careworn of late. The powers-that-be probably think he's too old and boring. Old and boring doesn't sell newspapers, I'm afraid. I should know I have to read enough of them for my course.' Jane fixed her mother with a wicked grin. 'Besides, I am the expert, or are you forgetting my two-point something years on a media studies course?'

Rosemary shook her head. 'Stephen's not old. He can only be about thirty-five.'

Misinterpreting her mother's protests, Jane threw the newspaper to one side and reached for her half-eaten slice of toast. 'When I said old, I didn't mean old-old as in geriatric.'

'I sincerely hope not! If you think Stephen Walker's old, goodness knows where that leaves me. What is it your brother says? Oldies, wrinklies and crumblies.' Reminded of a recent conversation with her eighteen-year-old son, Rosemary concluded, 'If, according to Ben, Stephen falls into the almost-oldie category, does that make me a wrinkly?'

Swallowing the remains of toast, Jane turned to her mother with a reassuring smile.

' 'Course not. Don't be daft! I never think of you as ancient. Being forty-two doesn't qualify you for a bus pass or a wheel-chair, yet. '

'That's a relief,' sighed Rosemary. 'And speaking of wheels, plural, in particular those parked in the drive, hadn't you better finish your packing and load up the car? If you do still want a lift? You'll miss your train if you don't get a move on. Have you seen the time?'

With a cry of panic Jane hurried away. It was only when they were driving to the station she was reminded of their earlier conversation.

'By the way, you never did explain why you had a touch of the vapours, just like one of your regency heroines?'

'Pardon?'

'Oliver's phone call. You got in quite a flap over Stephen Walker but never got round to telling me why. We became sidetracked, talking about age. Listening to your side of the conversation, not to mention the look of horror on your face at the time, would I be correct in assuming Oliver told Stephen you weren't too keen on his choice of hero?'

Concentrating more on negotiating the one remaining parking bay, Rosemary replied without thinking, 'Mmm. Oliver told Stephen I thought he was too old for the part of the hero, Edwin Crighton.'

This time it was Jane's turn to protest. 'Too old! How can Stephen be too old? You said yourself he's only thirty-five.'

With a resigned sigh, Rosemary switched off the ignition. 'Not you as well, Jane. I've already been through this with Oliver. If you must know, I never said Stephen was too old. I merely commented that I'd always imagined the part of Edwin being played by someone slightly younger. Oliver, being Oliver, immediately misinterpreted my reaction. The rest, as they say, is history.'

Jane studied her mother's face, which was filled with renewed despair. 'So it should be,' she said, trying to make light of the matter. '*To Love the Hero* is, after all, a delightful historical romance.'

Rosemary forced a weak smile. 'That's kind of you to say so. In the meantime, however, Oliver informs me that the *hero* in question is deeply offended by my remarks.'

'Good old Oliver.' Jane hauled one of her bags from the boot of the car. 'Never one to mince his words, eh? I'm not surprised Stephen was upset. Chill out, Mum. Your *hero's* renowned for being a bit prickly. He's had plenty of practice coping with the tabloid nasties. I'm sure he'll be able to cope with you.'

10

'I'm not nasty, am I?' Rosemary asked, following Jane on to the platform. She was about to add it wasn't Stephen who should be wary of her, it was the other way round, when she heard the almost unwelcome approach of the London train.

Before climbing aboard, Jane hugged her mother warmly. 'Don't worry. No one could ever describe you as nasty. I think you're lovely, so does Ben, only he's far too embarrassed to admit it. Did you know some of his new uni friends think you're brill? Anyway,' Jane finished hurriedly, while Rosemary was still puzzling over the word brill, 'It's a pity I can't say the same about the sweater. Promise me you won't wear it when you have lunch with Oliver. I know it was the last thing Dad bought you before he died, and you probably hang on to it for sentimental reasons, but it doesn't really suit you.'

Through misted eyes Rosemary waved goodbye, remaining on the cold and draughty platform until the train was out of sight. If it wasn't bad enough having had to say goodbye to both her offspring in less than twenty-four hours (she'd driven Ben to Sheffield the day before), Jane's parting words not only served to remind her of Gary's untimely death but also the forthcoming, and regrettably unavoidable, meeting with Stephen Walker.

Filled with a renewed melancholy, Rosemary returned home to a house now devoid of Christmas tree and decorations, luggage and excitable voices. Everywhere seemed so quiet and empty that it was several moments before she realized she'd walked from hallway to lounge without stumbling over a collection of shoes, books and assorted items of sports equipment. Then, when her gaze alighted on a favourite family photograph, she was no longer able to stem the flow of tears pricking her eyelids.

Taken little more than three years ago at her parents' holiday cottage in Norfolk, the photo captured a time when life had seemed so blissfully idyllic and secure. Gary, her husband, had been newly promoted to the board at Farmer and Butler, the publishers, Jane had been offered a place at university in London and Ben ... Rosemary gave a wan smile. Ben, as usual, had been her loveable, madcap teenage son.

Who then could have guessed that in three short months everything would have changed so dramatically? Gary's aneurysm, Jane leaving home for the very first time and Ben, desperately trying to take on his father's role as head of the family, and failing miserably.

With a long, lingering glance at the photograph, Rosemary brushed away a tear and straightened the frame, no longer jostling for space alongside numerous Christmas cards and festive candles. How strange that just like Ben's erstwhile mop of unruly hair (now worn stylishly short) her own life had also benefited from some serious pruning. Much as she'd loved Gary, it was only in recent months that she'd begun to realize exactly how overbearing and manipulative he had been during their twenty-year marriage. At least she was now free to make her own decisions (selling their executive-style home and moving to a much smaller one on a new development being the first) and choose her own clothes.

It was thinking of clothes and in particular Jane's parting comment about the sweater that filled her with concern. What should she wear for her lunch date with Oliver? Certainly not this unshapely thing, she determined, exiting the lounge to confront her reflection in the hall mirror.

Yes, her daughter had been quite correct in her assumption. Definitely not to her taste, Rosemary *had* chosen to wear the sweater because it was the last thing Gary had ever bought her. Though, as she reminded herself, while tugging the misshapen folds, it hadn't exactly come to light (complete with price tag) until several weeks after his funeral. Plucking a loose thread from one of the multi-coloured appliqué flowers, she still shuddered at its cost.

Moments later, pushing up the sleeves and pondering, as she'd done so many times in the past, why Gary should have bought a size fourteen, when she'd always been a twelve, Rosemary cleared the breakfast table, made herself a fresh pot of coffee and opened up the morning paper. What was it Jane had said about tabloid fodder?

Warmed by a feature on the fresh-faced boy band, celebrating their success at reaching number one in the charts, Rosemary soon found herself less kindly disposed towards a much-photographed young footballer, captured throwing a tantrum.

'Definitely tabloid fodder,' she murmured, closing the paper on the petulant teenager, only to be confronted by another disturbing photo. This time it was an angry mob of football fans, running riot. Likening all three photos to Ben's favourite classic western, *The Good, the Bad and the Ugly* – very ugly, in fact – Rosemary threw the newspaper into the bin.

At least not all football fanatics are hoodlums, she reminded herself, conscious of her son's passion for the game. '*Nor are all boy bands sweetness and light,*' Ben's voice echoed in her head. At least not if you'd been listening to the recent heated exchange between brother and sister during the Christmas vacation. Jane had been extolling the virtues, not to mention six-pack and brooding looks, of her latest idol, and Ben had been quick to point to a glossy magazine. On the cover was a less than complimentary photo of the aforementioned idol,

13

grappling on the pavement outside a smart London nightclub with a member of the paparazzi.

Somewhere in the shadows of her mind, Rosemary was convinced Stephen Walker had been snapped in a similar situation. Though hadn't they decided during breakfast that Stephen's bad-boy reputation was now a thing of the past? Too old and boring and perhaps looking somewhat careworn, Jane had even suggested.

'Perhaps a little bit careworn,' Rosemary suggested, recalling the last time she'd seen Stephen on a TV chat show. 'Old and boring? Never.' And she was still terrified at the prospect of meeting him.

Hoping for an exceedingly long delay before news of that dreaded first meeting, Rosemary was taken completely unawares by Oliver's late-night phone call.

'Rosemary, hi there. I hope I'm not interrupting the beauty sleep.'

'No,' Rosemary lied, suppressing a yawn while reaching for the bedside lamp.

'That's good, cos I've come up with a fantastic idea. Wouldn't it be great for you and Stephen to meet before rehearsals? Help you guys clear the air over lunch, so to speak.'

'Clear the air? Surely that won't be necessary? Oliver, I do wish you hadn't—'

'And Stephen would prefer Monday instead of the Friday, when I'd originally planned to meet you,' Oliver interrupted in his mid-Atlantic drawl, reeling off the suggested venue for their imminent lunch date. 'I told him you wouldn't mind.'

'Oh, did you?' Rosemary hissed into the now-silent phone, remembering only too well Oliver's penchant for ending phone calls and meetings before anyone had a chance to protest or air an opinion. Well, Oliver Duncan, for your information, this particular guy minds very much. She's even made a hair appointment in honour of the occasion! As for clearing the air, she thought, rearranging her pillows and duvet, all I can say to that is no wonder you're in films. I make one simple observation and you turn it into a full-scale melodrama.

Knowing it was pointless attempting sleep, Rosemary subjected a pile of cushions to a rigorous pounding and piled them behind her back. If she was this wide awake she might as well do something constructive. Revision of the synopsis and opening chapters of her latest novel seemed the perfect place to start. She'd already told her agent, Teresa, this was to be a feel-good romance set during the 1920s and 30s. Now, however, she began toying with the idea of a complete change of genre: a thriller, set on a film set, with the producer/director being the unsuspecting murder victim. Rosemary gave a wicked grin. In her mind's eye she could even visualize Teresa's astonished reaction.

Three revised chapters later, and her earlier ill humour dissipating, Rosemary concluded it was probably just as well Oliver had hung up when he did. In all the years that she'd known him, he had been a true and trusted friend. Because of that valued friendship she made a silent promise to avoid any further friction when they met Stephen for lunch.

Assorted cushions eventually discarded, Rosemary settled back against the pillows. Smoothing her shoulder-length hair back from her face as she did so, she caught sight of her reflection in the dressing-table mirror. A Monday lunch date meant an early-morning hair appointment was totally out of the question. Regrettably, Curl Up and Dye never opened on Mondays and she was desperate for a decent haircut.

*

Also desperate was Oliver, anxious that author and leading actor should get off to a perfect start. Greeting Rosemary warmly, he led her to the far corner of the bar.

'Stephen might be a bit late and suggests we start without him,' he explained, helping her to a chair.

'I certainly don't mind waiting,' Rosemary said, too polite to admit she was starving. There'd been no buffet on the London train. 'If you and I look through the menu beforehand, at least we can order the moment Stephen arrives.'

Nodding in agreement, Oliver summoned the waiter for aperitifs and they spent a pleasurable half-hour talking about old times. When another half-hour had passed, still with no sign of Stephen, Oliver began drumming his fingers against the table.

'I sure hope he arrives soon. I'm expecting a fax from the States. I told my secretary to expect me back by 2.30.'

Two-thirty, Rosemary thought, incredulous. She'd met Oliver at a quarter to one. They'd been sitting here for over an hour and even if Stephen did turn up now, they'd never be served in time. Chef was very strict about taking rushed, last-minute orders. It was an insult to his culinary prowess.

'Why don't I pop to the ladies' cloakroom?' she said brightly. 'Chances are the minute I'm gone Stephen will appear. If he does you can order for me. Anything quick will do. Especially if you've a 2.30 appointment.'

When she returned, Rosemary discovered Oliver beaming from ear to ear while patting somebody on the shoulder, although at first glance she took it to be a maintenance worker from the hotel (albeit a rather striking one at well over six feet tall) with untidy blond hair and dressed in jeans, fleece and trainers. Why should Oliver be greeting him so warmly?

It was only when Oliver murmured an aside and nodded in

her direction that Rosemary realized her mistake. Stephen Walker! Her breath caught in her throat. Jane was right. Definitely rugged and careworn – especially in his current attire.

Walking towards them, while at the same time pondering why Stephen hadn't worn a jacket and tie (as requested by the establishment), Rosemary was convinced Stephen was bidding Oliver goodbye.

'As you can see he's just this minute arrived but isn't stopping. A family crisis,' Oliver explained hurriedly. 'You'll just have chance to say a few words before he dashes off.'

Before Rosemary could even say hello, Stephen turned cool grey eyes in her direction and announced curtly, 'Ah, Miss Felden. There was me thinking I was last to arrive. Don't they say it's the fairer sex who are renowned for being late? If you'll excuse me. Another time, perhaps?'

Watching his abrupt and unexpected departure and heedless of the sheer disbelief flooding Rosemary's face, Oliver announced, 'Gee, I'm sorry. I never had chance to explain Romy Felden is only your pseudonym.'

'And I never had a chance to tell him it was *him* keeping us waiting, *not* the other way round' Rosemary seethed, under her breath. 'It must have been some family crisis.'

'How was Oliver and how was lunch? And what exotic culinary delights did they conjure up?' Jane questioned, ringing her mother two days later.

With her writer's mind linking the word conjure to magician, Rosemary reminded herself there had been nothing magical about Monday's meeting. Very briefly she described the fiasco that had been lunch and the less than palatable club sandwich eaten in the noisy, overcrowded bar.

'Food apart,' she conceded, 'it was really nice seeing Oliver again and catching up on old times. He always was a great favourite with the staff, when your father was working at Farmer and Butler.'

'Speaking of favourites,' Jane teased, 'I see your other favourite has come out of lurk mode. Stephen's making headlines again. At least in the London papers. I thought you might be interested so I've put the cutting in the post. Anyway, must dash. I've got a lecture. Bye.'

'My other favourite. You've got to be joking,' Rosemary said tersely, opening the newly delivered envelope. 'And some family crisis! Who's that with you, your niece?'

Acknowledging the fact that Stephen had at least bothered to smarten himself up for his 'family crisis' with the jeans, fleece and trainers of Monday lunchtime replaced by an extremely well-cut dinner suit, Rosemary threw the half-page newspaper cutting on the hall table in disgust.

Well-cut was right, she bristled, certainly as far as his extremely young and attractive dinner date was concerned. The journalist's report of Monday night's charity gala dinner made pointed reference to the fact.

'For once it wasn't infamous Stephen Walker who was drunk in charge,' the article began. *'But I can report his shapely companion certainly made up for them both. Refusing to comment on the unruly spectacle that prompted their early departure from last night's gala dinner, Stephen "To Love the Hero" Walker was anything but heroic as he manhandled the scantily clad Samantha into a waiting limousine . . .'*

Reminded that her own homeward bound 'limousine' had been held up for over an hour by delays on the line, Rosemary switched on her computer with a muttered, 'And I bet you never dined on a disgusting club sandwich!'

Distinctly unhappy at seeing *To Love the Hero* associated with such outrageous shenanigans, Rosemary refrained from ringing Oliver to complain. Knowing him he'd simply proclaim, 'But, *Rosemary*, any publicity is good publicity.' Far better to channel all that pent-up emotion into her writing instead.

Pleased with the morning's progress and the fact that she hadn't succumbed to another fit of pique (courtesy of Mr Walker), Rosemary emitted a curious smile and prepared a tray for lunch. How bizarre to think she actually had something in common with Stephen's female companion. While she would be using her own white damask napkin for its original purpose, Stephen's buxom bimbo had appeared to be wearing one!

Chapter 2

Arriving early for the first day of rehearsals, Rosemary looked about the busy studio. To her relief she saw Oliver almost immediately. Smiling broadly, he side-stepped a jumble of cables, cameras and lighting equipment and headed in her direction.

'Gee, I'm so glad you could make it,' he said, brown eyes twinkling, chubby arms extended in greeting. 'Sorry we had to alter the date. Gemma was convinced I should have given you more notice.'

'Gemma?'

'Gemma Parsons. My new assistant. She'll be taking care of you once filming gets under way. Last-minute changes and working to such a tight schedule means I might have to leave you to your own devices, I'm afraid.'

Last-minute changes? Rosemary puzzled. Did that mean Stephen Walker had changed his mind about playing the leading role and simply not turned up? He'd certainly been known to in the past.

Reading her mind, Oliver smiled diplomatically. 'Sorry to disappoint you. Stephen hasn't gone AWOL. I admit he hasn't arrived yet, but his co-stars Fergus Buchanan and Rachel

Masters are already on set. With or without Stephen, at least we're ready to roll.'

Registering Oliver's departing comment, 'Catch up with you later – perhaps dinner tonight?', Rosemary turned her attention to the day's proposed schedule. It was going to be a very long day.

Convinced dinner was extremely unlikely and that she'd prefer to leave the studios before it got dark, Rosemary looked up to find a young woman hurrying towards her.

'Miss Felden. How nice to meet you. I'm Gemma Parsons, Oliver's assistant. He's asked me to keep an eye on you and bring you a revised copy of the script. In case you hadn't noticed, he's already in a dreadful flap because Stephen hasn't arrived. At risk of getting my head bitten off, I did remind Oliver that Stephen's a law unto himself.'

'Or simply being his – er – usual charming self?' Rosemary replied, without expression.

Gemma nodded, as if reading Rosemary's mind. Bloody-minded would have been more appropriate in current circumstances. 'Let's just say Stephen Walker is what my mother calls a triple M. Mean, moody and mysterious. Perhaps it's a result of all the mean, moody and mysterious characters he gets to play. Whereas Fergus is an absolute honey.'

Spying the young woman's blushes, Rosemary presumed that just like her daughter, Jane, Oliver's assistant was also smitten by Fergus Buchanan. She had to admit that with his dark good looks and the merest hint of his native Scotland in a deep velvet voice, he was perfect for the role of Charles. But would Stephen Walker be the perfect Edwin? Rosemary Fielding aka Romy Felden was soon to find out.

*

During an impromptu and welcome lunch break, Oliver grabbed Rosemary by the arm. 'Quick!' he said, ignoring her notepad and pen falling to the floor. 'Come and meet Fergus and Rachel.'

Introductions completed, Fergus pointed to an unappetizing array of curling sandwiches. He grinned wickedly in Oliver's direction. 'See how well he caters for us, Miss Felden.'

For a brief moment Oliver's reply was lost on Rosemary. It was only when he patted his expanding waistline (no doubt referring to a private joke) that the bewildered author turned her attention to Rachel Masters.

To Rosemary's delight, Rachel was far prettier than she'd imagined and simply perfect for the part of Georgiana, her heroine. In a matter of minutes the two women were deep in conversation, completely unaware that they were being watched by an approaching solitary figure.

'Stephen. At last!' Oliver called. 'Come and say hi to Rosemary. I know you said you couldn't wait to talk to her about this project.'

I bet you couldn't! Rosemary thought, visualizing his hasty departure from the restaurant. At the same time, feeling an icy shiver between her shoulder blades, she recalled her earlier good intentions to remain civil. She extended her hand in greeting.

'How do you do, Miss Felden?' a cold voice murmured. 'I'm truly sorry to disappoint you.'

'Disappoint me?' she faltered, her hand held within his vice-like grasp.

'I understand you don't approve of me playing your hero,' Stephen began, his voice laced with sarcasm. 'However, would it make you feel any better to know that I offered to back out? Oliver wouldn't hear of it, I'm afraid. With the contract signed and sealed, as they say, it appears you're well and truly stuck with me.'

There was a stunned and embarrassed silence as Rosemary snatched her hand away. Thanks to Oliver completely misquoting her, she'd never expected Stephen to greet her with open arms. Then again, neither had she expected to be so humiliated. With a brave attempt at composure, she glared indignantly into steel-grey eyes.

'I didn't say that at all, Mr Walker. Oliver completely misunderstood my . . .'

Sensing Stephen was willing her to continue, Rosemary refused to be drawn. She was already getting into dangerous water. In desperation she looked towards Oliver, who far from offering support, appeared to be relishing the mounting tension. He fixed Rosemary with a cheeky grin.

'Take no notice of him, honey. Stephen takes great delight in unnerving people at first acquaintance. Perhaps it is true what they say about people from the north, particularly Yorkshire. That's where Stephen hails from, isn't it?'

'So I believe,' Rosemary said, her tone abrupt and earlier good intentions forgotten. 'Yet at the same time we mustn't forget he always puts his family first.'

Not giving Stephen the opportunity to ask what she was implying, Rosemary fixed him with an icy glare. 'I trust you enjoyed the gala dinner, Mr Walker. I'm truly impressed at how quickly you resolved your family crisis.'

Turning sharply on her heels, Rosemary hurried back to her corner of the studio, closely followed by Oliver. Retrieving her notepad and pen from the floor, he placed them on her lap.

'Aw, c'mon, Rosemary,' he said, his face registering concern, 'take my word on it. I know Stephen from way back and he's a real swell guy. OK, so he can sometimes be a bit brusque first time round. That's only because he received some bad press several years ago.' Oliver shrugged his shoulders. 'Seems the tabloids won't let him forget it, either. Believe me, honey, you'll really like him once you get to know him better.'

'Get to know him better?' Rosemary echoed, watching Oliver hurry away. 'For the moment I'd rather not, thank you!'

'Good. You are home,' Jane said down the phone to her mother. 'I'm all ears. Do tell . . . how did it go at the studio?'

'Oh, fine,' Rosemary lied. 'Oliver's still wearing those garish plaid jackets and—'

'Mum! Much as I like Oliver, the reason I'm ringing is to see how you got on with Fergus Buchanan. Is he as dishy in real life?'

'Very much so. Unlike someone else I could mention.' Recalling her frosty exchange with Stephen, Rosemary heard giggling at the end of the line. 'What's so funny?'

'I was about to say I hope you didn't go and upset Stephen further by tripping over his walking stick or zimmer.'

'His what?'

'Joke, Mum. You said Stephen was old, remember?'

'As if I could forget. Oliver's made sure of that. Anyway, what good would it do trying to explain otherwise? At the end of the day I'm sure Oliver knew what he was doing when he signed Stephen for the part. Let's face it, I only wrote the wretched novel. Seth Usher's been commissioned to write the screenplay and . . .'

'And?' Jane queried.

'And I almost feel as if *To Love the Hero* no longer belongs to me.'

'Like someone's stolen your baby? Is that why you sound so down?'

'Do I?'

'You do from here. Still, I expect it's only post-Christmas blues and the fact you're still missing me and Ben. By the way, has he rung?'

'Ben? You must be joking. He knows how to use the washing machine by now. It's also Rag Week committee night, or had you forgotten?'

'Which means he's probably got his head in a bucket,' Jane volunteered. 'I suppose if you're lonely you could always get a dog.'

Rosemary frowned. Was she lonely? She didn't think she was. Admittedly there were times when the house felt horribly empty and quiet but she'd had to get used to that since last September. As for missing Gary. . . . he'd been dead for three years. Three years in which to mourn, move to a smaller house and make a career for herself as a local theatre critic and mid-list novelist. No, she definitely wouldn't describe herself as lonely.

'If you are thinking of a dog don't forget Sarah's border collie,' Jane's voice broke into Rosemary's train of thought. 'Isn't she expecting pups? Why not ask if you can have one? Better still, go and pick one out for yourself? Sarah must get bored stiff, stuck on that remote farm. I'm sure she'd love to hear about Stephen Walker. I bet he's not nearly as rude as you make out.'

Not bothering to explain that Sarah (her old school-friend) was perfectly happy living in Wales with her sheep-farmer husband and their three teenage children, Rosemary said goodbye. It was one thing her daughter suggesting that she buy a puppy, quite another being reminded of her encounter with Stephen Walker.

'Hmm. Two fairly *close* encounters,' she corrected softly, while dialling Sarah's number, all the while reminded of flint-grey eyes and long blond hair, concealing a very determined set of jaw. 'I hardly dare think what will happen on the third.'

'So, that's my news all up to date. What about yours?' Rosemary queried, after chatting to Sarah for a few minutes.

'Oh, Ro. What an exciting life you lead,' Sarah replied, ignoring the question. 'Will you be going to the studio again?'

'Oliver did suggest a return visit before they all head off on location. I'm not so sure I can cope with a repeat performance.'

'Rubbish!' Sarah scolded. 'Ro Fielding, sometimes I think you're as daft as our sheep. You may have said something you now regret, but Oliver was also at fault for repeating it. As for Stephen .. You and I both know the press were always giving him a hard time, particularly when his career was first taking off. We all did stupid things when we were young.'

'Did we?'

'I certainly did. Or had you forgotten? The summer we came to Wales for that camping holiday, once we'd finished our A levels. I fell down and twisted my ankle. Haydn came to my rescue and now look at us – an old married couple with three kids and hundreds of sheep.'

'Surely you don't regret it? I thought you and Haydn were really happy together?'

'We are and I love him and the children to bits. It's simply that I sometimes wish I'd met him later. You know . . . had a chance to travel a bit or do something wildly exciting, like my famous friend, and perhaps write a book?'

Rosemary smiled. She'd never be so vain as to describe herself as famous or her life wildly exciting. 'My dear Sarah, knowing you as I do, I think you'd find life as a writer an extremely solitary occupation.'

'Nonsense! Just take your visit to the studio. That wasn't being solitary. And if you are invited on set again, I want you to promise me you'll go. Better still, take me with you.'

'Why? So that just like my love-struck daughter you can drool all over Fergus Buchanan?'

'Lord, no! He's far too perfect for the likes of me. What you see is what you get with Fergus B. What I'm dying to know, and I'm sure you are too, only you won't admit it, is what really lurks behind that deeply furrowed brow of the deadly serious but deliciously sexy Stephen Walker. As for Jane suggesting you get a dog, I'm afraid all our puppies are spoken for. Even if they weren't, I still wouldn't let you have one.'

'Why ever not?'

'Because what you need, Ro Fielding, is a man.'

'And you, Sarah Thomas, are a hussy!' Rosemary teased. 'In spite of that, you're still my very best friend.'

Chapter 3

Relieved to see the dreary month of January drawing to a close, Rosemary was both surprised and delighted when Ben and Jane came home to celebrate her birthday. She insisted on taking them to the local bistro for lunch.

'That's not quite what we had in mind, Mum,' Jane said, helping her mother with her coat. 'Our intention was to treat you for a change. Still, at least we can cook for you tomorrow and you won't have to do a thing. Ben and I have everything under control. Correction. I have everything under control, little brother can simply follow orders!'

Rosemary raised her eyebrows in disbelief. Jane's little brother had grown like a weed during the past five months. The thought of him taking orders was distinctly amusing. Nonetheless, it would be nice to have their company, especially on her birthday.

Leaving Ben to fetch drinks from the bar, Jane escorted her mother to a table by the window. Their order completed, she reached for a breadstick, snapped it in four and popped one piece into her mouth.

'That reminds me Mum,' she said, inadvertently arranging a breadstick letter 'N' on the red and white check tablecloth.

'How's the great north-south divide?'

'The what?'

'The working relationship between you and Stephen. Is the atmosphere still as frosty, or do I detect signs of a thaw? Before we left I just happened to notice his photo on the desk in your study.'

'Sorry to disappoint you, Jane. If you'd looked more closely you'd have noticed that was just one of a pile of publicity stills. Gemma sent them a couple of days ago.'

'I don't suppose you've got a spare photo of Fergus?' Jane asked, moving her breadstick 'N' to make room for Ben's arrival with the tray of drinks.

Ben groaned. 'Don't tell me she's still drooling over that Fergus fellow. We're not having that regency stuff all through lunch, are we?'

'For your information, Ben, it's that so-called regency *stuff* that's keeping us both at university.' Jane fixed her brother with an angry glare.

Momentarily consumed with guilt, Ben mumbled, 'Sorry, Mum,' and offered Rosemary a breadstick.

'And I'd better apologize too, cos I've been teasing Mum about the great north-south divide,' Jane continued in response to her brother's raised eyebrows. 'Before you ask, I mean Mum's aversion to Stephen Walker. Stephen's from the north and Mum's from the south.'

'Can you call fifty miles north of London south?' queried Ben.

'Does it matter?' Rosemary replied. 'Fergus Buchanan's from the north of Scotland and I like him a lot. I'm only sorry I turned down his dinner invitation.'

Jane practically choked on her breadstick. 'You did what? But why?'

'Because I had a better offer. My son and daughter came home to celebrate my birthday.'

Spying Jane's crestfallen face, Rosemary explained. 'Actually it wasn't Fergus who invited me, although he will be there. The invitation came from Oliver. He's taking some of the cast and crew out for a meal before they head off on location.'

On Sunday, with the smell of garlic pervading the kitchen, followed by loud banging noises interspersed with the occasional, 'Oh, Ben!', Rosemary fled to the relative peace and tranquillity of her study.

Peaceful it might be, she thought, sifting through a pile of papers, but it was in the most frightful muddle. Not only was her desk covered in pages of script, but there were the assorted photo stills, the first hundred pages of her new novel, numerous as yet unanswered letters and the usual, unwelcome pile of bills.

'Looks like you could do with a secretary,' Jane said, poking her head round the door to announce lunch was ready.

Rosemary sighed and shook her head. 'Definitely not a secretary. I couldn't afford one. Besides, I work better on my own. What I really need is more storage space. Although at the moment I'd be happy enough just to find somewhere for these.'

These, Jane observed, were three piles of newly assorted papers. 'Why not use Dad's old briefcases?' she suggested as they made their way to the dining room. 'If I remember correctly, he had at least four. I'm sure you kept them. Do you know where they are?'

'I know I never threw them out because your father had such expensive taste. Ben, didn't I suggest you use them for your A level projects?'

'Yes, and I refused.' Ben grinned, taking a deep slurp of his wine. 'Walking into sixth form with a leather briefcase in my hand would have been so uncool.'

'Point taken,' Rosemary conceded. 'So can you remember what you did with them?'

Ben thought long and hard while stabbing at a forkful of spaghetti carbonara.

'They're probably at the bottom of that old toy chest in my bedroom. I'll have a look after lunch if you—'

'No way!' Jane broke in. 'After lunch, for your information, means helping me clear up that mess in the kitchen.'

While culinary chaos gave way to ensuing calm, Rosemary sat on the edge of Ben's bed. Surrounded by boxes of Lego, Star Wars figures and numerous Action Men in various guises, she eased them carefully on to the floor, save for a solitary decapitated Action Man. She then turned her attention to each of Gary's four briefcases.

Assuming them all to be empty, she was surprised to find a concealed zip fastener compartment stuffed with an assortment of old theatre tickets, credit card slips and hotel bills. Numb with shock, Rosemary stared at them in acute disbelief. Hurt, anger and disgust filled her very being as she fought back a sob and the onset of nausea.

'When did he...? How could he...?' she whispered, unaware of Jane's presence in the open doorway, before slipping quietly away to warn her brother.

'Oh, shit! I completely forget they were in there,' Ben called out, dashing upstairs two at a time, closely pursued by his sister. 'I put them there just after Dad died cos I didn't want Mum to find out and...'

'Now I have?' Rosemary challenged, her voice catching in her throat. 'Am I to understand you both knew about this?

You knew about your father and this . . . this . . .'

'Other woman?' Ben finished for her. 'Yes, we did, Mum. We thought it was better if you didn't know. Jane said you'd find out eventually. Of course, as usual, she's right.'

Giving her brother's arm a reassuring squeeze, Jane joined Rosemary and Ben on the dishevelled bed. 'We . . . um . . . didn't want you to know you'd been betrayed, Mum.'

Betrayed! The cruel word with all its connotations cut through Rosemary like a knife. Making a grab at the assorted papers, she re-examined theatre tickets for productions she'd never seen, bills for clothes she'd certainly never worn and as for the seemingly endless credit card slips for perfume and duty free . . . 'So many of them,' she said, disbelief flooding her face. All those so-called business trips and extravagant gifts on her husband's return. A means to appease his guilt no doubt, she thought bitterly. All remnants of her life with Gary. Only it wasn't just her life, was it? It was also a life he'd shared with some other woman.

'Did I know her?' she asked, as if searching for clues amongst the scattered papers. 'Tell me. I need to know. My God! Was it Laura? Is that why Laura left to go to the States?'

Ben's arm curled protectively about his mother's shoulders. 'No, Mum. You didn't know her. Believe me, that's the truth.'

'Is it?' Rosemary pleaded, stifling a sob. 'Is it really?'

Marginally comforted when Ben and Jane both nodded, Rosemary reached for her handkerchief and dabbed at her red-rimmed eyes. For one truly awful moment she'd thought it might be Laura Carr, Gary's former business partner and her very dear friend, who was now living in America. She shuddered at the thought. That would have been far too painful to bear.

Later, while Ben and Jane were packing their overnight bags, Rosemary decided to go for a walk. Watching her leave, Jane placed a restraining hand upon her brother's elbow.

'No, Ben. Let her go. It will probably do her good to get out of the house for a while. She'll be OK – you'll see.'

'You really think so? Jesus! How could I be so bloody stupid? I could kick myself for leaving that stuff in the brief-case. I'd meant to chuck it out ages ago. I suppose I just forgot.'

'In a way I'm glad you did. It's about time Mum knew what a liar and a cheat Dad was. Admit it, it hasn't been exactly easy trying to keep quiet about that little secret over the years. Besides, Mum can't go on mourning him for ever.'

Ben scowled. 'Some little secret! Anyway, she won't have to now.'

'No, thank God, so let's hope she can continue to make a new life for herself. Perhaps even marry again?'

'Marry? You've got to be joking! She hasn't even got a boyfriend, has she? And isn't she a bit. . . ?'

'Don't you dare say old. In case you hadn't noticed, Ben Fielding, our mother is an extremely attractive woman. I accept she could probably do with one of those makeover thingies and begin by chucking out half her wardrobe. That's only because Dad was such a control freak, insisting on choosing most of her clothes.'

'Hey! You don't think he did that deliberately, do you? You know, choose old-fashioned things for Mum while he bought all that trendy stuff for his lady friend?'

'Hmph! Some lady. And you could have a point there, although I wouldn't go so far as describing Mum's clothes as old-fashioned.'

'Maybe not,' Ben said, trying to remember the contents of

his mother's wardrobe. His mother always looked smart and neatly dressed, even when they were staying at their holiday cottage in Norfolk.

Meanwhile, Jane gathered together a pile of books in preparation for her forthcoming dissertation. Deeply reflective, she placed them on the hall table. If asked for her opinion, she would describe her mother's clothes as stylish and quietly classic. It was almost as if her father hadn't wanted anyone else to notice his attractive wife. Deciding to keep this thought to herself, she went on to say, 'The more I think about it, the more I'm convinced that awful appliqué sweater Mum persists in wearing was never meant for her.'

'That's not funny,' Ben retorted, seeing Jane's face break into a smile.

'Don't look so hurt, little bro. I wasn't thinking of that. I was thinking of a recent magazine article we were discussing at uni.'

'What about?' Ben called, running to answer the phone.

'That women are supposed to be in their sexual prime when they reach their forties.'

Spared her brother's blushes, Jane decided to put the kettle on ready for their mother's return.

Taking Ben and Jane to catch their respective trains, Rosemary saw little point in further discussion relating to Gary's infidelity. Hadn't they suffered enough already? Instead, trying to remain philosophical and put on a brave face, she listened to Ben's plans for attending numerous sporting events in Sheffield.

'Don't forget you're also there to work,' she said. 'Which reminds me, did you remember the Charles Dickens?'

Ben was reaching into his padded jacket for his portable

CD player. 'Charles Dickens? What do I want with Charles Dickens? Jane's the one doing media studies and English. I'm reading geography. Remember?'

Pulling in to the station car park, Rosemary replied, 'I merely asked because of the message on the telephone pad in the hall. It was definitely written in your horrid, spidery scrawl. Was there something you forgot to tell Jane?'

Spying the look of abject horror on her son's face, Rosemary realized something was dreadfully wrong. 'Ben?'

'Oh shit! I don't believe it. Twice in one day. First that bloody briefcase business and now this.' In response to Rosemary's look of disapproval, Ben mumbled, 'Er . . . sorry Mum. Actually, the message was meant for you. Will you please ring him? He said to say it was urgent.'

'Who? Charles Dickens? I don't even know a Charles Dickens!'

'Course you don't,' Ben said sheepishly. 'But you do know an Oliver and that's Charles Dickens, isn't it? They made it into a film and Harry Secombe sang 'If I Ruled The World.'

'And if I ruled the world, Ben Fielding, I'd—'

'Think it, don't say it, Mum. Somewhere in that scatterbrain head of his there must be something resembling a brain. He did get three grade As and a B for his A levels, remember.'

Jane pulled a face behind her brother's back and zipped up her fleece. 'And please don't wait for our trains to come in. Best get off home and ring Oliver. You never know, he might be planning another dinner party.'

Once more alone with her thoughts, Rosemary rang Oliver and then turned her attention to Gary. At least what was left of him. With grim determination she scoured the house and, beginning with the loathsome appliqué sweater and tell-tale contents of the briefcase, gathered everything together and headed for the garden.

Knowing only too well a proper bonfire was out of the question (borough council regulations) and hoping the neighbours wouldn't complain, she piled everything into the wheelbarrow, pushed it to a far corner near the compost heap and lit a match. What could be more perfect, she thought with a faint glow of satisfaction. Tomorrow she would place what remained of Gary's ashes on the roses. It would be a fitting tribute to his memory.

Watching myriad flames curl and lick the side of the wheelbarrow, she wiped a mixture of smoke and tears from her eyes. 'Happy Birthday, Rosemary,' she gulped, fresh tears coursing down her cheeks.

Chapter 4

With Monday's post came a bulky envelope from Oliver (the reason for his phone call) thus distracting Rosemary from her cruel discovery of the previous day. Inside she found yet more pages of revised script and Oliver's hastily scribbled note. He was having second thoughts about Seth Usher's screenplay. Not only that, Stephen – yes, Rosemary had read the note correctly – was also expressing similar concerns. He'd even suggested that Oliver consult Rosemary to arrange a meeting ASAP.

'*Progress good. Weather awful. Will call you,*' Oliver had concluded.

Looking out on to stormy, gun-metal skies, hardly daring to think of her next meeting with Stephen Walker – would that be stormy too? – Rosemary remembered last night's phone call from Sarah. The weather in Wales had been dreadful. And they were in the middle of lambing.

'Ro. I'm so sorry. I've never forgotten your birthday before. The weather's simply awful. We're struggling with early lambs. In fact, the kitchen is full of them, and Haydn's asleep on his feet, poor love.'

At the sound of Sarah's voice, Rosemary had burst into

floods of tears. Telling her the sordid tale of Gary's affair, she'd been surprised by silence at the end of the line.

'Sarah? Are you still there?'

'Yes.'

'And have you nothing to say?'

'Oh, Ro . . . you mean you never suspected?'

'Are you saying you knew too?' Rosemary cried, aghast.

'Not exactly. Haydn and I just sort of guessed. All those last-minute business trips and book fairs didn't seem right somehow.'

'Not forgetting all his bloody little treats and surprises,' Rosemary announced bitterly. 'There was me thinking he was so thoughtful and generous, when all along it was only his guilty conscience.'

'And I'm feeling guilty about your birthday. So, now that you've had a jolly good cry, blow your nose, fetch your diary and tell me when you're coming to stay.'

Explaining that it was completely out of the question (she was waiting for Oliver's summons), Rosemary did her best to convince Sarah that the last thing she and her overworked husband needed was a neurotic woman going through a mid-life crisis.

'Don't be stupid,' Sarah scolded in her adopted, lilting Welsh accent. 'You and I are the same age. We've done every-thing together. I'm certainly not experiencing a mid-life crisis and neither are you. In fact, I absolutely forbid you to. Now then – oh, bugger! A lamb I've been nursing has just escaped from his bed in the bottom of the Aga. I'll be back in a tick. Don't go away.'

Moments later, when Sarah returned to the phone, she was laughing. 'Right,' she called, out of breath. 'Caught him, the little devil. Now, as you've had time to think about it, tell me what you've decided to do about your mid-life crisis, while I've been chasing lambs?'

'Nothing,' came the feeble reply.

'Nothing? Are you sure?'

'Positive. I've decided to put it on hold until I come to see you.'

'Then make sure you come soon. In the meantime. I'll send some photos of the kids. You'll hardly recognize them now. They're getting quite grown up.'

Promising she would, Rosemary had also promised to follow Sarah's instructions for interring Gary's ashes first thing in the morning.

'Roses are far too good for him!' Sarah declared angrily.

'Then I suppose the Dicentra might be more appropriate.'

'The what?'

'That's bleeding heart to you,' Rosemary explained, with a chuckle.

'Oh, all right, clever clogs. I was forgetting you're a budding Alan Titchmarsh. As for bleeding heart, I don't think you'd approve of my response to that one, especially in relation to Gary. Far too Anglo-Saxon. Let's just say that as far as your dear departed husband – or at least what's left of his belongings – is concerned, we've got a lovely muck heap in the corner of our yard.'

Knowing full well that a trip to Wales was completely out of the question, Rosemary did at least follow Sarah's chain of thought. Twenty minutes later she found herself unceremoniously dumping Gary's remains on the compost heap. With a satisfied smile, she took great delight in mixing him in with assorted vegetable peelings, old teabags and some rather dead and very smelly, rotten Chrysanthemums.

Hurrying indoors from darkening skies, already heavy

with rain, her thoughts turned immediately to cast and crew of *To Love the Hero*. If, according to Oliver, they were still filming on the Yorkshire moors, then Stephen Walker would also be getting rather wet.

In response to Oliver's earlier request, Rosemary spent several days working on the script and in particular Stephen's role of Edwin Crighton. Satisfied that she'd dealt with all the specified requirements, including Stephen's queries, she also determined to resolve any outstanding hostilities. As she'd remarked to Sarah, she didn't usually have problems communicating with people, did she?

Still in the same positive frame of mind on Friday afternoon, she was congratulating herself on the finished result, when Oliver rang from his mobile.

'Rosemary. Hi! I'm in the car and we're heading back to London. Say, I know it's short notice but can you get to the studio tomorrow? Stephen's still insisting we discuss this tower scene together.'

Rosemary stifled a sigh. What could she say? When she'd last spoken with Gemma about a further proposed visit to the studio, she'd expressly asked for any day other than a Monday. How could she therefore object if Oliver wanted her there on a Saturday? Reluctantly agreeing to his request, there was a sudden tremendous crackle down the line. For a fleeting moment the phone went dead.

'Brother! Did you hear that?' Oliver cried, delighted, once they'd been reconnected. 'Some thunderbolt! By the way, you'll love the storm scenes we shot. Ain't no need for wind and rain machines here. Anyway, glad you can make it to London. Why not stop over for once? I'll take you to supper.'

Supper with Oliver and a night in the capital. It was

certainly a very tempting proposition. Perhaps she could visit the National Gallery or even the new exhibition at the V&A before leaving on Sunday? And if she planned her wardrobe now, she could pack this evening and catch the first train to London in the morning. Wonderful! Only it wasn't, Rosemary thought miserably. There was still the problem of the promised new haircut.

Marginally comforted that at least the salon would be open until late and the adjacent arcade boasted some fairly decent clothes shops, Rosemary reached for the phone.

'Curl Up and Dye,' a deep, nasal voice intoned.

'Hello. It's Rosemary Fielding. I appreciate it's very short notice but I was wondering if Vickie could fit me in for a trim and blow dry, either this evening or early tomorrow morning?'

'I'm ever so sorry, Mrs Fielding. Vickie's got flu. She won't be back until Wednesday at the earliest.'

'Oh dear. Poor Vickie. Then perhaps an appointment with someone else?'

The someone else at the end of the line sniffed and blew her nose hard. ' 'Fraid not. It's not only Vickie who's poorly. If you'll pardon the pun we're all dying here and also double-booked. Lord knows how we're going to cope. How about the end of next week, that's if Vickie's back?'

Half-expecting to see hordes of germs leap-frogging through the handset, Rosemary declined and hung up. Having reluctantly turned down Sarah's offer of a trip to Wales, she had absolutely no intention of turning down Oliver's invitation of a weekend in London.

Arriving at Euston early on Saturday morning, Rosemary saw to her surprise a seemingly endless array of heart-shaped balloons, gifts and long-stemmed red roses. February 14th, St Valentine's Day and she hadn't even realized. Then again, why should she? It had been three years since she'd received Gary's choice of an over-elaborate card and his usual delivery of two dozen red roses.

Rosemary gave an involuntary shudder. Yet more evidence, if needed, of her husband's guilt. Most men would simply buy one dozen red roses. Gary Fielding, however, newly christened the bastard, always had to buy two.

Still smarting at the thought of Gary's duplicity, Rosemary made her way to the studio where Oliver was already waiting.

'Thanks for coming in so early, and at such short notice. Stephen's really keen to speak with you. I'll tell him you're here.'

'There's no need. He already knows. We met in the corridor. As for being keen to speak to me, he practically ignored me.' Against her better judgment, Rosemary in turn ignored Oliver's raised eyebrows. 'I admit it probably wasn't helped by some idiot calling him "grandad" as I passed by. Really, Oliver, I do wish you'd kept my remark about Stephen's age to yourself, instead of making it quite so public.'

'Hey! Hold your horses! I'll put it right with Stephen once and for all. OK?'

'I doubt whether he'll take any notice, so please don't bother on my account.'

'I won't!' Oliver snapped, his tone unusually sharp. 'For your information, I need to get this production in the can and completed on schedule. There's a lot of money at stake here. Do I make myself clear?'

Unable to explain why she was feeling so edgy, Rosemary watched Oliver march over to Stephen and take him firmly by the arm. He spoke only for a moment, his voice raised, and nodded in her direction. Fully expecting Stephen to follow Oliver's example and storm off set, she saw to her amazement he was heading towards her with two cups of coffee.

'Miss Felden. Would you like a coffee? I'm afraid it's only from that awful machine in the corridor but at least it's hot.'

Strangely curious, Rosemary looked up to where he towered above her. Where was the indifferent gaze he'd thrown at her only a short while ago? And did she also detect the merest glimmer of a smile in his eyes?

'I believe I owe you an apology,' he began. 'Oliver has explained about the earlier – shall we say – misunderstandings. In turn however, I think I should also explain why I've perhaps been so . . . er . . . unsociable. The truth is I've been extremely worried about my goddaughter and the company she keeps. Without prior consultation her parents left her in my charge and the result has been unmitigated disaster. No doubt you've seen the papers? Everyone else appears to.'

Storing the words *unsociable, goddaughter* and *unmitigated disaster* in her head, along with the tabloid photo taken at the charity gala, Rosemary refrained from further comment. Not a good time, she told herself, watching Oliver reappear from his vantage point behind a cherry picker.

Nodding approval, he caught Rosemary's eye, only to be distinctly put out when Gemma arrived, carrying a bundle of assorted envelopes and packets.

'I've brought your post, Stephen. Looks like they all still love you,' she teased.

Saying nothing in reply, Stephen waited for Gemma to leave before ripping open the largest of the envelopes. Spying an expensive satin and lace-edged heart, he gave a slow, cynical smile.

'Funny thing, Valentine's Day. Don't you think so, Miss Felden? All this money spent on cards and presents and I don't even know who they're from.'

'Perhaps you should be pleased somebody cares?'

'Perhaps,' Stephen said with a distracted smile, opening another envelope. 'I expect I'm right in thinking your husband cares enough about you to send at least a dozen red roses.'

'Not exactly. In fact, Gary always used to send two dozen. This year however, he sent me a rather unique present from the grave.'

'From the. . . ?' Stephen began, registering only too late the tears welling in Rosemary's eyes, before she hurried away. Damn it! How could he be so bloody stupid? Ages ago Oliver had told him that Romy Felden's husband had died of a heart attack or something similar. If only he hadn't been so preoccupied with Samantha, his spoilt brat of a goddaughter, he probably would have remembered and approached the subject with caution.

'Well done, Stephen,' he said, his voice laced with sarcasm as he threw the unopened bundle of cards into a nearby bin. 'Oliver's going to love you now. Try explaining away that little scenario.'

That night over supper, Oliver apologized for his earlier irascible behaviour.

'And I'm sorry too,' Rosemary said, telling him briefly about Gary.

With a rueful shake of the head, Oliver refilled her glass. 'I can't say I'm surprised. There were always rumours in the New York office. For what it's worth, he didn't deserve you, my dear. So, as I sense you'd rather not talk about Gary, shall we talk about what you and Stephen made of the script instead?'

Taking a deep gulp of wine, Rosemary concluded now was not the time to tell Oliver they hadn't decided anything at all. In fact, the only making that had taken place was her making a complete and utter fool of herself.

Several hours later, mellowed by good food, excellent wine and Oliver's fatherly concern for her welfare, Rosemary returned to her hotel.

'Now all I need is a warm bath and a good night's sleep,' she murmured, stepping into the empty lift.

Once in her room, she kicked off her shoes, massaged her aching feet and was in the process of heading for the bathroom when she was halted by the ringing of the phone. Frowning, she hurried to answer it. She certainly wasn't expecting any calls at this time of night and she'd only just left Oliver in the taxi.

'Miss Felden. There's a man from the florist's in reception. Shall I send him up?'

A florist? At this time of night? Surely not. Then again, this was London. It was also a highly respectable hotel.

'No. Don't send him up. Tell him I'll come down. But first I must find my shoes,' she announced into the now-silent receiver.

Stepping nervously from the lift, Rosemary's stomach gave a lurch. She'd recognize those broad shoulders and distinctive physique anywhere, even before he turned round. Stephen Walker!

'Mr Walker?'

Turning slowly, Stephen moved towards her. In his hand she saw he carried a single, long-stemmed white rose, exquisitely wrapped in clear cellophane and tied with a simple red bow.

'I've tried everywhere for a red one,' he said simply. 'Unfortunately they were all sold out. However, I got to thinking this is perhaps more appropriate with me coming from Yorkshire. Don't they associate white with peace?'

Completely taken aback, Rosemary struggled for something to say. Memories of distant lessons with her favourite history teacher, Mrs Sims, sprang to mind. The Wars of the Roses and in particular the white rose of York and the red rose of Lancaster.

With a nervous smile, she clasped the rose in her hand. 'As you've probably gathered from my accent, Mr Walker, I'm certainly no Lancastrian. But I'll happily accept your offer of peace.'

Conscious of the young receptionist, who was becoming even more interested in this flowery exchange of blossoms and words, Rosemary motioned towards the nearby brasserie. 'We never did finish our coffee this morning. Do you . . . er . . . have time for one now?'

Stephen nodded, breathing a deep sigh of relief. He certainly hadn't been expecting such a gracious acceptance speech. In fact, all the time he'd been waiting for her to return, he'd half expected her to throw the rose at him in disgust.

Sipping deliberately at her coffee, Rosemary studied Stephen across the table. Unless she was very much mistaken, he was looking absolutely exhausted.

Seconds later, when Stephen's eyes met hers, she felt herself colour. Unable to hold his gaze, she gave an embarrassed smile. To her utter amazement he smiled in return, completely transforming his whole appearance.

Dispensing with small talk, Stephen progressed to more immediate concerns, namely the tower scene from *To Love the*

Hero. He'd read the book, more than once, and studied the screenplay repeatedly. Yet somehow he was convinced Seth Usher had totally missed the point of the plot. 'I was wondering,' he said without warning, 'if you'd care to discuss it over dinner on Monday night?'

'Monday? I . . . hadn't planned to stay until Monday. I was going home tomorrow.'

In answer to her unspoken question, Stephen replied, 'And I shan't be here tomorrow. I'm going to Sheffield, which means an early start.'

'Sheffield? What a coincidence. Ben, my son, is studying at the university. At least I hope he is.'

'Lucky Ben. I'm told it's a great place for it. Of course, I never had the opportunity myself.' For a fleeting moment, Rosemary thought she discerned a flicker of emotion play at the corner of Stephen's mouth. Had she detected a tiny chink in his armour?

'About Monday,' he asked, hurriedly changing the subject. 'Would it matter if you stayed another day?'

'Well . . . no. I suppose not.'

'Good. That's settled. I'll pick you up at 7.30. Now, if you'll excuse me. One way and another, it's been quite a week. In case you hadn't noticed, Oliver can be a bit of a slave-driver at times. Oh Lord! Please don't tell him I told you so. We don't want any more misunderstandings, do we?'

To her relief, Rosemary saw that Stephen was smiling again. Helping her from her chair he accompanied her to the lift. 'Goodnight, Miss Felden,' he said softly, reaching for her hand. 'I hope you enjoy your Sunday in London.'

'Goodnight, Mr Walker. Have a safe journey to Sheffield. I take it you will be driving?'

Stephen gave a curious grin and nodded, watching her step

into the lift.

Her mind racing, Rosemary clutched at her rose and said without thinking, 'What should I wear? I mean . . . where shall we be eating?'

'Don't worry,' came the bemused reply, sensing her eyes were on familiar jeans, fleece and trainers. 'I promise to smarten myself up a bit. We'll eat Italian if that's OK?'

'Italian would be wonderful and thank you again for the rose,' she called after him, before the lift doors whispered shut and he was gone.

Touched by the sheer simplicity of Stephen's peace offering, Rosemary felt like pinching herself. The single delicate bloom, so pure and untainted in its clear cellophane wrapper, somehow reminded her of Snow White in her glass case, waiting for her prince to come. Looking ahead in the mirror, she shook her head and smiled. She was certainly no Snow White. And in jeans and well-worn fleece, neither was Stephen a prince. But he had at least proved he was human.

Freshly bathed and ready for bed, Stephen's rose was the last thing Rosemary saw before switching off the bedside lamp. What was it he'd said earlier? Something about it being quite a week.

Beginning with Gary's ashes. and ending with this exquisite rose, she supposed in a way he was correct. 'Well, Stephen Walker,' her sleepy voice echoed in the darkness. 'On that at least we both agree. So where do we go from here?'

Chapter 5

Waking early next morning, Rosemary stretched and yawned sleepily. Padding barefoot towards the window, she pulled the cord on the heavy brocade drapes, releasing as she did so a flood of wintry sunlight into the room. It was then she caught sight of Stephen's rose. Pure and white, neither a dream nor a figment of her imagination, it was still there. What had prompted Stephen to buy it? Was it really a peace offering or had he simply felt sorry for her? Whatever the reason, its sheer simplicity had moved her far more than the dozens of red roses ever sent by Gary.

Showered and dressed, wearing the suit she'd worn to the first day of filming, the reality of staying in London began to take hold. She couldn't possibly wear the same clothes today *and* tomorrow evening. Originally planning to stay only one night, she'd considered her neatly tailored suit, plus change of blouse, sweater and undies, more than adequate. Sadly, not adequate enough for a dinner date with Stephen, she told herself. Alarmed by such a prospect, she concluded there was only one solution. Today she would window shop, tomorrow she would buy. Before that, however, lay the delights of the Victoria and Albert Museum.

Beginning with the Regency costumes, Rosemary was in her element. What fun it was to make comparisons with the clothes contained in the cabinets and those worn by the cast of *To Love the Hero*. Silently admiring the simple empire line dresses in fine silk and muslin, she moved on to two exquisite male forms dressed in coats of fine broadcloth, satin breeches and silk waistcoats. It could even be Stephen and Fergus, she mused, unaware of the stranger standing by her side.

'Aren't they simply divine?' a woman's quiet voice began, bringing her back to reality. 'And wouldn't it be adorable if all men dressed like that today.'

Rosemary nodded and smiled. 'Lovely, yes. But perhaps somewhat impractical.'

'Especially impractical for the men I know,' came the reply. 'I'm Suzanne Milburn, by the way. And in case you hadn't already guessed, I'm a long way from home. Born in Pittsburgh, Pennsylvania, but now living in New York. However, I just love your V&A and come here every time we're in London.'

'We?'

'Oh, I'm on my own at the moment. Wally, my husband, is still at the hotel. He doesn't share my enthusiasm for men in satin breeches and silk waistcoats,' Suzanne giggled. 'I'm therefore allowed to drool completely undisturbed and we meet up here for lunch. Say, if you're on your own, why not join us?'

Rosemary hesitated only briefly before introducing herself. Ordinarily she would have declined such an invitation but there was something about Suzanne's open, honest face that reminded her of Oliver. Besides, she'd already discovered they shared a love of all things Regency.

Admiring the rest of the collection together, Rosemary turned up her nose at the heavy crinolines, boned bodices and bustles that followed. 'I'm not surprised so many of them died of consumption. The poor creatures couldn't even breathe in those corsets.'

Suzanne gave a wry smile and patted her stomach. 'Hmm. Well, I can assure you they're considerably finer and a great deal more comfortable to wear these days. Not that you would know, Rosemary. You're far too young and slim to need them.'

In the restaurant, a genial Wally thanked Rosemary for taking care of his wife and keeping her company. Explaining that he worked in real estate and that they liked to visit England twice a year, he went on to describe his wife's love of historical fiction.

'Suzanne just loves your Jane Austen and Regency romances. Our bookshelves back home are simply full of them. Why, if she buys any more I guess we'll have to move house.'

'I guess we might,' Suzanne teased, patting her husband's hand. 'Particularly after this trip. What I don't have to guess about is Rosemary. She's exactly like one of my favourite Jane Austen heroines.'

Rosemary blushed. 'Gracious, Suzanne! I'm far too old to be a heroine. Besides, I have two grown-up children.'

'Really? Oh well, that's as may be, my dear. But back there in the costume department, seeing you gaze longingly at the figure in the blue tailcoat, you could have been Miss Elizabeth Bennet gazing into the mysteriously brooding eyes of Mr Darcy.'

Amused, yet not wishing to offend, Rosemary refrained from further comment. She was almost twice Elizabeth Bennet's age.

After lunch and saying goodbye, Wally handed Rosemary his business card. 'If you're ever in New York, promise me you'll call.'

'Actually, I do have a friend who's forever begging me to go and stay. Laura works in publishing—'

'Which means she must also be very busy,' Suzanne broke in. 'All the more reason for giving us a call. We promise to take good care of you while she's working.' Linking her husband's arm, she added as an afterthought, 'By the way, why not have your hair cut like the girl in the blue muslin?'

The girl in the blue muslin? Baffled, Rosemary watched them walk away until she was suddenly reminded of their earlier conversation. She'd told Suzanne not only was she staying in London because of a dinner engagement, but also that she had to buy something suitable to wear.

'Then you must go for a complete new you,' Suzanne had insisted. 'Spring is only round the corner. Each spring and fall I go the whole hog: new hairstyle, new wardrobe, the lot. Believe me, my dear, it works wonders for the morale. Just you try it.'

If only I could, thought Rosemary, reminded that Jane and Ben's university fees usually took priority. Student accommodation wasn't exactly cheap in either London or Sheffield. Even with the offer of using her friend Laura's London flat while she was working in the States, and the success of *To Love the Hero*, Rosemary still acknowledged that a 'new you' twice a year was virtually impossible. On the other hand (with Laura having insisted that Jane make use of her vacant apartment for the next six months) just this once shouldn't upset her bank manager, should it? Buying a postcard of the girl in the blue muslin frock, Rosemary left the museum to go window-shopping.

First thing on Monday morning and with Suzanne's recommendations still fresh in her mind, Rosemary approached the hotel's beauty salon with trepidation. Completely nonplussed, the stylist examined the recently purchased postcard. Used to clients producing cuttings from newspapers and magazines, this was the first time she'd been shown a style from the early nineteenth century.

'Of course not quite like that,' Rosemary explained hurriedly. 'I thought perhaps something ... er ... short and feathery?'

'Mmm. I think I know what you mean,' the stylist said, draping a cape around Rosemary's shoulders. 'It's not unlike some of today's hair fashions. What had you in mind for the colour?'

'Colour? I hadn't even thought about colour.'

Turning to one side, the young woman reached for a colour chart. 'Lowlights would be nice. You know, nothing too drastic and they're far less severe than bleach. They'd also enhance your natural colouring.'

Peering into the mirror, Rosemary found herself wondering how you enhanced natural mouse. And before she had a chance to enquire, she found herself succumbing to a tightly fitting skull cap and something resembling a crochet hook. Resisting the urge to wince at the occasional twinge of discomfort, while at the same time suppressing the frequent desire to sneeze, she watched in horror as deft and nimble fingers applied shades of copper and gold to her hair.

Rosemary bit her lip and looked away. What on earth would Jane and Ben say if they saw her now? She was only too grateful that they couldn't when the cap was eventually removed, the colour washed off, and a small pair of scissors were set to work, snipping and trimming at her shoulder-length hair. Catching sight of it cascading to the floor, Rosemary gasped and reached for the nape of her neck.

'Don't worry,' a voice assured. 'It's going to look lovely. I think you'll be pleasantly surprised. You look years younger already.'

'Heavens, I don't want to look like mutton dressed as lamb.'

The stylist laughed. 'Trust me. You won't do that either.'

Totally unconvinced, Rosemary watched another chunk of hair fall to the floor. Even if the girl wasn't speaking the truth, it was far too late to do anything about it now. She was therefore both surprised and delighted with the finished result. Her hair, now a delicate combination of copper and gold, had been swept forward and gently fingered into place. Not only was it extremely flattering, it also enhanced her grey-green eyes and made her features more defined.

The stylist reached for a hand mirror. 'Well . . . what do you think?'

For a moment Rosemary was speechless. 'I – I think it's lovely,' she said, turning to catch the reflection of the back of her head in the mirror. 'Though it's certainly going to take some getting used to. Is that *really* me?'

Reassured that it was, Rosemary was instantly reminded of Stephen. His hair was now far longer than her own. Oh dear, what would he think of her? More importantly, looking like this, would she even have the courage to face him tonight? Several hours later, heavily laden and possessed of a new-found confidence, she hailed a cab in Regent Street and returned to her hotel.

'Rosemary Fielding! What have you done?' she scolded, spying first her reflection in the mirror and then all the assorted shopping bags scattered on the floor.

Fingering a wayward strand of hair from her forehead, she reached for the largest of the bags, her heart giving a flutter when her fingers touched the layers of tissue within. Such extravagance for something so plain and simple. A *something* that had felt oh, so right from the moment she'd slipped it on, even without the assistant's positive cooing.

'The perfect little black dress,' she murmured, her eyes sparkling as she held the garment against her. Apart from at Gary's funeral, she'd never worn black. Gary had always insisted it didn't suit her. Now she didn't give a damn.

For one fleeting moment, Rosemary toyed with the idea of ringing Wales. Perhaps even tell Sarah about Stephen's rose and his totally unexpected dinner invitation? Then again, perhaps not, she thought. Sarah was still in the middle of lambing and doubtless trying to prepare the children's tea. Wouldn't it be better to ring later? Just in case . . .

'*Just in case what?*' a tiny voice enquired.

'In case I don't go.'

'*Don't go?*' It was almost as if Sarah was in the room with her. '*Why, Ro Fielding, stop being such a wimp! Put yourself first for once. Of course you'll go! Forget about Gary. Forget about the money you spent today. Just get out of that sensible suit and those awful shoes and let yourself go for once. God knows you deserve it!*'

With a desperate attempt at ignoring the butterflies in her stomach, Rosemary kicked off her shoes, unbuttoned her jacket, gave one last lingering look at her numerous purchases and headed for the bathroom door.

Showered and wearing glamorous new undies, she turned her attention to her make-up bag. Out with the old and in with the new, she told herself firmly, and emptied a selection of well-used lipsticks, eye pencils and blushers into the padded brocade bin. At least Suzanne Milburn would be proud of her.

Examining her brand new make-up palette with its myriad colours, Rosemary was reminded of a patchwork in miniature. Could she really bring herself to scar the delicate surfaces with an assortment of brushes and sponges? If only Jane were here to offer some advice.

Convinced that Jane would simply say, 'Just don't overdo it, Mum,' Rosemary opened a small pot of foundation with trembling fingers.

Make-up accomplished, it was time for the dress. Yes, she told herself, the three-quarter length sleeves had been a good idea. At least they didn't show her goosebumps. Completing the outfit with a pair of chunky gilt-knot earrings and contrasting silk scarf, which she draped across her shoulders, Rosemary slipped her feet into elegant black patent slingbacks, picked up the matching handbag and new hip-length jacket and made for the door. It was 7.25. Stephen had said 7.30. She didn't want to be late.

It was only when she pressed the button for the lift she remembered the personalized copy of her book and, hurrying back to her room, heard the unexpected ringing of the phone.

'Miss Felden? It's Stephen Walker. I'm so glad I've caught you in time. I'm dreadfully sorry but I—'

'Can't make it?' Which is the polite way of saying you've changed your mind, Rosemary thought miserably, trying to dismiss all thought of time and money spent on getting ready for this evening.

'Can't make it?' Stephen repeated flatly. 'No. It's not that. It's my car. It's packed up on me, I'm afraid. Which means I shall be a bit late ... probably by at least twenty minutes. Would you mind waiting in reception rather than the bar? Then I'll ask the cabbie to keep the engine running while I pop in to collect you.'

'Oh, I see. Yes. Don't worry, I'll wait there instead. Mr Walker, before you go – there is just one thing. Do you think you could call me Rosemary? Miss Felden makes me feel like a maiden aunt.'

'As long as you call me Stephen,' he replied.

Hearing him laugh before he hung up, Rosemary relived her initial disappointment when she thought he wasn't going to make it. Her spirits soared. He hadn't rung to cancel. He would be here in twenty minutes!

Moments later a frisson of renewed panic filled her very being. What would he say when he saw her? What would she say when she saw him? More to the point, what would people think, seeing them together?

This is simply ridiculous, she chastized. It was only hunger and nerves getting the better of her. OK, so perhaps after today's miracle transformation she didn't really look like his maiden aunt, but she was still seven years older than Stephen and could hardly be considered his type. Taking a deep breath and trying not to think of the recent newspaper cuttings, Rosemary headed for the bustling reception.

It was a further fifteen minutes before Stephen came rushing in, his eyes scanning the milling throng.

'Stephen,' she called softly, emerging from the far corner.

'Rosemary. I'm so sorry. When my car wouldn't start and finding a cab was virtually impossible . . .' But he got no further. Stephen Walker stopped in his tracks, unable to believe his eyes. Then, swiftly taking control of the situation, he offered her his arm.

'The traffic was simply horrendous,' he continued, leading her outside to the waiting taxi.

Saying nothing, Rosemary quickly noted that he'd kept to

his word. No jeans, no fleece and no trainers. Instead, he was wearing a finely knitted black rollneck sweater, black trousers and a deep sapphire blue jacket. Exactly the same colour as the exquisite tail-coat she'd admired so much at the V&A. She shuddered at the memory.

'I'm truly sorry,' Stephen began. 'You're obviously frozen from waiting by the door for so long. Once the cab got stuck in that almighty traffic jam I realized there was nothing I could do. I knew I should never have relied on Mabel.'

'Who's Mabel?'

'My car. Or should that be what passes for one? I'm surprised you haven't heard about her. She's a standing joke at the studio. We've been together for years but she's been letting me down just lately. Poor dear, she certainly doesn't like this cold weather.'

I know just how she feels, Rosemary thought, wriggling her toes to bring them back to life.

Grateful for the welcoming warmth of the restaurant, Rosemary followed a waiter to a table in the farthest corner.

'I hope you don't mind being tucked away,' Stephen said, helping her off with her coat, which he passed to the waiter. 'Only it gets quite noisy later on, particularly when the theatres close. It's also far away from prying eyes.'

'I take it you speak from experience.'

'I do. For the simple reason it's one of our favourite haunts. By our I mean Jake De Havilland. We come here to celebrate when we have plenty of work, or commiserate when we don't. Jake's an old friend. Just like Mabel, we go back a long way. We were even in rep together.'

Jake De Havilland? Rosemary reflected. Hadn't Jane mentioned a Jake De Havilland only recently? 'Am I correct in thinking that's not his real name?'

Stephen grinned, revealing a row of even white teeth. 'Absolutely, Miss Marple. His real name is Jack Lockheed, like the aircraft, but he thought he stood more chance in the acting profession if he changed his name. Jack became Jake and the Lockheed, ... it's self-explanatory really. He picked De Havilland from an aircraft magazine and he's never looked back.'

'It's certainly amusing.'

'As amusing as Romy Felden? A little bird called Oliver told me you are also known as Rosemary Fielding.'

'Ouch! I suppose I asked for that?'

'I'm sorry,' Stephen said quickly. 'I didn't mean to sound sarcastic.'

'That's all right. No offence taken and you do have a point. I suppose Jack and I each had our reasons for changing our names.'

This time it was Stephen's turn to look bewildered. He paused, hoping for an explanation.

'Well, Jack presumably changed his name to draw attention to himself, whereas I changed mine for anonymity.'

'Now I'm even more confused,' Stephen said with a disarming smile.

Looking across the table, Rosemary saw that he was studying her carefully. Just like Saturday when he'd given her the rose, the fine lines at the corners of his eyes creased into a smile. He was also still waiting for an explanation.

'It's a very long story.'

'That's OK. We've got all evening, haven't we?'

All evening. From the sensation in her stomach, she could only conclude the myriad butterflies had collided. Rosemary demurred. She so wanted to enjoy this evening but not if it meant talking about Gary.

'Of course, if it's too painful . . .' Stephen said, pursing his lips. He didn't want to upset her again, especially as Oliver had already deemed it necessary to inform him not only of Gary's treachery but also the money and extravagant gifts he'd lavished on his mistress.

'No, it's all right,' Rosemary assured. 'And I'll try to keep it brief but if you do get bored, please tell me.'

'I promise.'

Deciding to deal with her husband's death as quickly as possible, Rosemary began. 'Gary was on his way back from a book fair when he was taken ill. By the time the ambulance reached the hospital, however, it was already too late. As you can imagine, the aneurysm came as a dreadful shock to all of us. Initially, I coped extremely badly, which was why Sarah, my old school friend, suggested I go and stay with them. Sarah and her husband have a remote hill farm in Wales.'

'So you decided to write a book about sheep farming?' Stephen teased.

Rosemary shook her head and smiled. 'No. But Sarah did suggest I try my hand at writing a novel as it was something I'd always aspired to.'

Stephen was watching the waiter pour their wine. 'You surely don't expect me to believe it happened just like that?'

'Not exactly. But you'd probably find the minor details tedious.'

'Try me,' he said, raising his glass in her direction.

Pressed into explanation, Rosemary described the writing competition run in conjunction with Gary's old firm of publishers and a national magazine. Her decision to use a pseudonym, and the address of the family cottage in Norfolk, was in case anyone at Farmer and Butler recognized her name or address.

Meeting Stephen's baffled gaze across the table, Rosemary toyed with the stem of her wine glass. 'Unlike your friend Jake, I don't read aircraft manuals. I borrowed the name of my parents' holiday cottage in Norfolk instead.'

'Which is?'

'Romany Fields.'

Deep furrows formed in Stephen's brow. 'How does Romany Fields become Romy Felden?'

'I did warn you it was quite a saga.'

'Perhaps you should write a book about that too?'

'I doubt if anyone would want to read it. Quite simply, my father used to call me his little gypsy or his little romany. He greatly admired the writing of George Borrow ... Romany Rye and Lavengro. Anyway, as I could never pronounce romany it always came out as romy.'

Stephen nodded. 'And the Felden?'

'That's how Freda and Harry have always pronounced my surname.'

Stephen grinned a lop-sided smile. 'I'm with you so far on the Romany Fields but now I'm hopelessly lost. Who are Freda and Harry?'

'Sorry, I should have explained before. They look after the cottage in our absence. Fielding in Norfolk dialect, at least the way Freda and Harry pronounce it, always comes out as Felden.'

Watching Stephen digest her potted history to date, Rosemary speared an olive. 'So tell me, unlike your friend Jake, shall I presume Stephen Walker is your real name?'

'Afraid so. Sadly, I don't possess Jack's vivid imagination and my parents never had a holiday cottage. Born plain

Stephen Walker, I remain plain Stephen Walker.'

Hardly plain, particularly from where she was sitting, Rosemary wanted to add. Instead she felt it far safer to ask about his previous day spent in Sheffield.

Recounting his long overdue visit to see his father, who was recovering from a particularly unpleasant attack of flu, Stephen mentioned he was also consumed with guilt because filming was taking up so much of his time.

'Perhaps that's why Mabel wanted a night off?' Rosemary suggested. 'Especially if you subjected her to that long drive yesterday. Although it is a journey I do with Ben, I confess the traffic in the centre of Sheffield simply terrifies me. Not only that, I always seem to get lost.'

Sipping thoughtfully at his wine, Stephen's eyes met hers across the table.

'Perhaps I can help there. Next time I go, why don't I give you a lift? Born and bred in Sheffield, I know the place like the back of my hand.'

Mention of his hand prompted Rosemary to study the hands that had not only presented her with the rose but also guided her gently to the waiting taxi. Feeling a warm flush at her throat, she was grateful for the subdued lighting and the approaching waiter heralding the arrival of their meal.

For the remainder of the evening and much to her surprise, she found herself totally at ease in Stephen's company. Talk of his time spent in rep soon gave way to their current working relationship with Oliver. At length the conversation invariably progressed to Ben and Jane.

'Yet another coincidence,' Stephen remarked. 'Not only is your son studying in Sheffield, but also it looks as if your daughter's living in a flat not far from where Jake and I used to have lodgings.'

'And for that I have to thank Laura. She's another dear friend. The flat was her London bolthole before she was promoted and sent to America. Although only big enough for one, I have been known to squeeze in on occasions when I've visited. This time, however, thanks to Oliver, I'm wallowing in the lap of luxury.'

Further mention of Oliver reminded Rosemary that they still hadn't discussed *To Love the Hero*. Wasn't that why they were having dinner together, to discuss Stephen's concerns? Reaching for the signed copy of her book, Rosemary passed it across the table.

'I thought you might prefer a hard cover as opposed to a paperback. And . . . if you'd care to discuss the scenes that are troubling you, I shall be only too happy to oblige.'

Thanking her profusely, Stephen flicked through the pages to the relevant chapters. 'It's just a gut reaction I have, that's all. As I mentioned to Oliver, I'm convinced Seth Usher has completely misinterpreted that part of the plot. I'd certainly welcome your opinion.'

Some time later, declining a second cup of coffee, Stephen looked at his watch and frowned. It was far later than he realized and with Oliver having scheduled an early morning shoot, he really ought to be asking for the bill.

'Is there anything wrong?' Rosemary asked. 'I thought we both agreed the tower scene should be . . .'

Stephen shook his head. 'No, it's not that. I've been puzzling over something you said earlier. Something about your father calling you his little romany. Why was that?'

'That's because I was never still and my hair was always wild and unkempt. A typical *raggle-taggle gypsy-o*, Father always used to say. Are you by any chance familiar with the song?'

'I am. In fact, we had to learn it at school. Although, from where I'm sitting you look anything but. Please don't think me rude, Rosemary, but your hair – it's . . .'

'Far too short?'

'Gracious, no! It's simply that you gave me quite a shock when I arrived at the hotel. Usually it's the male of the species who has short hair and as I've grown mine for the role of Edwin Crighton . . .' Stephen hesitated and fixed her with a smile, while pushing back his thick blond hair from his face. 'What I'm trying to say is that I think short hair really suits you. You don't look anything at all like a maiden aunt.'

Returning to her hotel, Rosemary studied Stephen's profile. In the semi-darkness of the taxi his features appeared strong and strangely reassuring. Tonight, instead of being rude and arrogant, he'd been charming and attentive. The perfect host in fact and quite possibly the perfect *hero*. To her surprise, she'd even been able to look him in the eye. Unlike their first embarrassing encounters, when she'd tried so desperately to avoid him. With her thoughts winging away to her first day at the studio, she was taken completely unawares when a high-performance car cut dangerously in front of them.

'Bloody idiot!' The taxi driver called, swerving to avoid an accident. Glancing quickly in his rear-view mirror, he saw Rosemary slide across the seat into Stephen's arms. 'Sorry about that, guv. Is the lady OK?'

'Rosemary?' Stephen asked.

Conscious of the fact he was still holding her close, even though the taxi had righted itself, Rosemary felt her throat go dry. She could even smell his aftershave and the atmosphere in the rear of the cab seemed almost electric.

'Yes. Yes, I'm fine. Just a little shaken, that's all. I suppose I really ought to have worn my seatbelt but the hotel's only around the corner, isn't it?'

Stephen nodded in reply as the hotel came into view. Moments later, declining his offer of seeing her to her room, Rosemary thanked him for a delightful evening and watched as both the taxi's rear lights and Stephen's silhouette disappeared into the cold February night air.

Minutes later, with all manner of thoughts twisting and weaving their way through her head as she unbuttoned her jacket, Rosemary couldn't help but recall the closeness of his body as he'd steadied her in his arms. As for the subtle perfume of his aftershave, she was convinced she could smell it, even now. Closing her eyes she breathed in deeply. Saturday night's dinner date with Oliver had been one thing (he was, after all, just a good family friend), but for this evening spent with Stephen . . .

Oh, you fool! she thought angrily, her eyes snapping open. You poor deluded fool letting your mind wander like that. How could you be so feeble-minded? You've obviously had far too much to drink.

Ignoring the fact that she'd had only two glasses of wine all evening (too much red wine gave her a headache), Rosemary forced herself to think of the endless tabloid photos of Stephen with assorted blondes and brunettes, most of them wearing little more than a table napkin or a slither of fabric held together with safety pins.

And do you honestly think he'd be interested in the likes of you? a voice echoed cruelly in her head.

As if in reply, Rosemary choked back a sob and clasped a hand to her breast. It wasn't her head that ached, it was her heart. She hadn't felt like this for more than twenty years.

Chapter 6

Returning home by train, Rosemary had ample time for contemplation, the vision of last night still fresh in her mind. Stephen with his sweep of long blond hair and expressive, searching eyes, filled with anxiety lest he should upset her again; and Stephen with the strong yet gentle hands, holding her close in the taxi.

Rosemary's own small hands fluttered briefly across her overnight bag. There, just beneath the zip fastener, lay his rose. Oliver had been right all along. Stephen was *a nice guy*. She had to admit she'd certainly enjoyed his company. What puzzled her now was how she had ever found him so objectionable.

With the resulting euphoria from her London trip lasting well into the afternoon, Rosemary prepared an early supper, reached for a lap tray and took it through to the lounge. Switching on the television for the early evening news, she discovered nothing had changed in her absence. Politicians, both in government and opposition, were still trying to outwit each other over yet another ministerial scandal and the royals were still making headlines.

Thank goodness I'm not in the public eye, she thought,

closing the curtains against darkening skies. For the most part authors remained anonymous – unlike someone else she could mention.

Rosemary bit her lip reflectively, mindful of Stephen's early forays on to the front pages of the newspapers. During dinner he'd made little reference to his earlier notoriety and she'd been far too polite to pry.

'Just a warning to wrap up warm tomorrow and not to travel unless it's absolutely necessary,' the weatherman's kindly voice urged from the corner of the room. *'We're expecting heavy falls of snow.'*

Snow? It hadn't looked like snow when she'd arrived at the station, or when she'd drawn the curtains. Still, the weather man had been known to get it wrong before. Who would ever forget the October hurricane?

Before locking the house for the night, Rosemary stepped outside and breathed in deeply. Sure enough, the air did smell of snow, prompting her to recall Gary's familiar words of contempt.

'Don't be so ridiculous, Rosemary! Of course you can't smell snow in the air. It's impossible.'

But it wasn't, she'd pleaded, because Freda and Harry always said the same thing.

'Freda and Harry are just a pair of simple yokels,' Gary had snorted derisively. *'Full of old wives' tales and no sense at all. I ask you, who in their right mind would choose not to have a washing machine?'*

It had been pointless trying to explain that Freda enjoyed doing things her way. With her old-fashioned copper on the boil, scrubbing brush and bar of green soap at the ready, Freda was in her element. Primed for her regular Monday assault on the week's washing, she would sing hymns at the top of her voice.

Beginning with 'Morning Has Broken', swiftly followed by 'All Things Bright and Beautiful', it was strange how she'd launch into 'Fight The Good Fight' whenever Harry's blue overalls came into view. At this point the well-worn bar of soap would invariably escape Freda's vice-like grip and go scudding across the quarry-tiled floor, swiftly followed by Freda's sing song cry of, 'Blas'ed soap! There it goo agen.'

With a smile and humming the opening strains of 'Fight The Good Fight' to herself, Rosemary climbed the stairs to her bedroom. Once there, she opened the window and leaned out. Yes, she could definitely smell snow.

Too tired to read, her thoughts turned to Gary and Stephen before she switched off the bedside light. Gary, she knew she would never see again, leaving her with countless bitter-sweet memories. As for Stephen . . . would she be seeing him again? Taking comfort in the knowledge that she would be making at least one more visit to the studio (she'd promised to take Jane), Rosemary made a mental note to ring her daughter first thing in the morning. No doubt Jane would love to hear all about Jake De Havilland.

Waking with a start, Rosemary sat up, her heart thumping in her breast. What a dream! Or should that be nightmare? Wiping tiny beads of perspiration from her top lip, she real-ized she was shaking. While the prospect of Stephen invading her slumbers hadn't given rise to panic, it was Gary's unwel-come appearance that had.

Stephen had been standing on a bridge wearing the blue tailcoat and satin breeches (exactly like those at the V&A) while Rosemary, dressed in blue sprig muslin, made her way towards him. In the middle of the bridge, however, and determined to bar her way, was Gary. Dark eyed and scowling, his face cruelly sinister, his intentions were abundantly clear. Stephen and Rosemary would not be allowed to meet. In a display of anger, Gary reached out, determined to wrench Rosemary from Stephen's waiting embrace. Helpless and defenceless, she was flung against the parapet to await her fate.

Shuddering and gasping in the choking and enveloping darkness, Rosemary fumbled for the bedside lamp. She must get up. Get some air. Get a drink of water. Anything. There was no way she could go back to sleep now. Every time she closed her eyes, she saw Gary's cold, leering smile.

Deciding she would feel more comfortable downstairs, she paused at the landing window. No wonder the house appeared enveloped in an eerie stillness. Everywhere was a blanket of white. It was snowing.

Transfixed by the ghostly flurries drifting silently to the ground, Rosemary was glad she wouldn't be travelling anywhere tomorrow. If it carried on snowing like this it would be quite deep by morning. Pulling her dressing gown closer, she marvelled at the filigree patterns spiralling against the window and the solitary street light beyond.

'It could almost be Narnia,' she said out loud, her author's imagination going into overdrive, half-expecting Lucy and the others to appear. There were no children's voices, however, just the faint purr of a solitary car and a honey-pale sweep of headlights ploughing through a swirl of snowflakes.

By morning, just as she'd expected, everywhere was a carpet of white and the view across open fields enchanting. For the moment it was perfect but if they did go ahead with the proposed new ring road, what then?

Despite heavy, swollen skies no more snow fell that day or

the next. On the third day, as if by magic, it had all but disappeared. Only across the distant fields did she discern small pockets of white where once there had been snowdrifts. Tempted by brilliant sunshine and ignoring the one black cloud in the distance, she ventured into the garden with her washing.

Breathing in deeply while lifting her face to the bright February sunshine, it wasn't long before she turned her attention to the newly opened blossoms at her feet. Rosemary smiled, fascinated. Why, they were just like little people. On her right were swathes of crocus, bold and bright and upright, like soldiers, while in the far corner, under the ornamental cherry, clumps of white and green-tipped snowdrops hung their heads like demure Regency virgins.

Moving round the tiny garden, Rosemary discovered yet more delights. Hiding beneath last season's dark spotted leaves of Pulmonaria were tiny pink and purple buds. There were even bright green spikes of late-flowering daffodils. Peeping out from the rich, dark soil, they were like fledglings in a nest. Deeply moved by the newness of life, she felt a lump rise in her throat. A new year, barely two months old, and already the onset of spring. What could be more perfect? Even the robin and wren had resumed their long-standing battle over territorial rights. The entire garden was defying the snow to return.

When the hard crunch of tyres on gravel brought an abrupt end to round one between robin and wren, Rosemary looked at her watch. Probably the postman, she decided, waiting for the familiar revving of the engine as he slammed the van into reverse and shot back down the drive. Oliver had promised to send some photos taken during location in Yorkshire.

To her surprise there was no squeal of brakes or agonized

crunching of gears. Instead there was only the persistent ringing of the doorbell.

'Oliver being cautious, I expect,' she announced to the robin, now perched quizzically on an upturned flowerpot. Hurriedly wiping her feet on the doormat, she ran to the front door.

'Stephen!'

'Hello, Rosemary. I hope I'm not disturbing you. Interrupting the writing or anything?'

'N-no. I simply wasn't . . . um . . . expecting you that's all. I thought you were the postman. You know, special delivery. Oliver told me—'

'Put like that, I suppose I am. Special delivery, I mean.' Stephen grinned in response to her bewilderment. He held out a large brown padded envelope. 'These are for you. Photos from Oliver, I believe.'

Rosemary gaped, amazed. Her mouth had gone suddenly dry, her stomach lurched and she felt rooted to the front doormat. 'You surely haven't made a special journey all this way simply to. . . ?'

'No. Oliver didn't need me today. I heard him ask Gemma to send these special delivery. And as I'd already promised to drop something into a friend, who works in the vicinity, I offered to bring them personally. I hope you don't mind.'

'N-no. Not at all. Do you have an appointment?' she asked, her gaze alighting on the piles of boxes on the front and rear passenger seat of his car.

Stephen appeared momentarily taken aback. 'What? Oh, no. He simply said to pop in any time.'

'Does that mean you have time for a coffee?'

'Coffee would be wonderful. Only if I'm not holding you up. Were you going out?'

'I've already been out,' Rosemary said, wishing she was wearing anything other than her gardening coat and boots. 'Out in the garden to be precise. Hence the less than fashionable attire. I was hanging out the washing and became sidetracked, checking on the bulbs I planted last autumn. It's amazing how everything's suddenly bursting into life, despite the snow.'

Following her through to the kitchen, Stephen watched her remove her coat and boots before stowing them away in the utility room. He then turned his attention to the kitchen window and the neatly tended garden beyond.

'I have to confess I don't know a great deal about gardening myself. My dad's the green-fingered member of the family. Right proud of his allotment, he is. We never had much of a garden at home.'

Rosemary detected a slight burr of Yorkshire dialect when he spoke of his father and also the merest touch of unease when he spoke of home. Come to think of it, she wasn't feeling particularly at ease herself.

Recalling to mind her vivid nightmare three nights ago, she felt a rush of colour to her cheeks. To make matters even worse, when she quickly turned her back on him to fill the kettle, she saw that her hands were shaking. Dear God, she prayed silently. Tell me this isn't really happening.

Five minutes later, taking the tray from her arms as she nudged open the door to the lounge, Stephen was directed to a small coffee table and one of two two-seater sofas arranged on either side.

'What a good idea,' he remarked, placing the tray on the table, his eyes resting admiringly on the pale apricot chintz.

'As you can see the room's far too small for the traditional three-piece suite. I discovered these fitted in better and made more use of the space.'

Stephen waited for Rosemary to sit down. She hesitated, as if pausing before a strategic move in a game of chess. Either way she felt vulnerable. Should she suggest he sat by her side? She'd already noticed the familiar scent of his aftershave (just as she had in the taxi). Or should she direct him to sit opposite her, where they wouldn't be in such close proximity?

Deciding the first option was safest (she could at least avoid direct eye contact), Rosemary quickly ascertained that sitting nearest the door also meant a means of escape. Opening the front door and finding him on the threshold had caused panic enough.

Willing her hands to keep still, Rosemary poured coffee into fine fluted china, passed him a cup and motioned to the cream and sugar. Stephen declined both.

'Your friend. What line of business is he in?'

'Friend? Oh, you mean Brian,' Stephen replied hurriedly. 'Lithographs, printing and reprographics. I don't understand much about it myself but I gather he's just bought himself a new digital press. He's renting a unit at Swallow Park. Do you know it?'

Rosemary shook her head. Swallow Park was on the other side of the ring road. With so many small businesses setting up over there, it was worse than Hampton Court maze.

There was a pregnant pause in the conversation, broken only by the ringing of the telephone. Grateful for a reason to leave the room, Rosemary hurried to answer it. To her dismay it was a wrong number. Replacing the receiver, she noticed that the one black cloud in the sky had not only trebled in size but also appeared to be hovering overhead.

'The washing!' she cried, hearing the first spots of rain dash against the window-pane.

Disregarding Stephen's offer of help she ran outside, only to find him following her to the back door.

Minutes later, trying to conceal her recently purchased silk and lace undies beneath a bath towel, Rosemary saw Stephen walk towards her. In acute embarrassment she backed away, catching her leg on the laundry basket.

'Oh, drat!' she said without thinking. 'Now I've laddered my stocking.'

'And here's one you dropped earlier,' he said, with a wry smile, passing her a single sheer, black stocking that had escaped the hastily collected laundry. Stephen nodded in the direction of the tiny ladder creeping above her knee. 'Can you do anything about that? Don't they recommend nail polish or something?'

Glad of a second chance to flee, Rosemary excused herself and went upstairs.

Intrigued, Stephen watched her disappear. Somehow she hadn't looked the type to wear stockings. Most women these days wore tights. Certainly her legs, or at least what he'd seen of them while helping her in and out of the taxi, were shapely enough for stockings.

Returning to the lounge, Stephen remembered that today when he'd arrived, there hadn't been a hint of leg in sight. Rosemary's neat, trim figure had been completely enveloped by a thick gardening coat, tweed skirt and knee-length boots. She also appeared extremely flustered by his presence. What is it you're also trying to hide? he asked himself, looking enquiringly at the surrounding family photographs, tasteful watercolours and exquisite porcelain.

In her absence Stephen studied a photo of Rosemary and her two children. Jane, he observed, was a plumper version of her mother with a cloud of hair surrounding her head like a halo, while Ben presumably took after his father. Looking distinctly uncomfortable in shirt and tie, Ben's eyes and short cropped hair were of a deep chestnut brown.

Aware of the faint smell of nail polish, Stephen turned from the silver-framed photo to find Rosemary standing in the doorway.

'Would you like some fresh coffee?' she asked, reaching for the pot.

'No, thank you. My sister's always telling me I drink far too much of the stuff. What I would like, however, is for you to stop rushing about like a mountain goat – albeit a very attractive one, I hasten to add.' Patting the cushion by his side, Stephen said softly; 'Do come and sit down, Rosemary. I don't bite, you know.'

Rosemary gulped nervously, still unable to meet his penetrating gaze. Was it really that obvious?

Taking her hand in his, she heard Stephen say, 'Oliver told me how much you value your privacy so I'm deeply sorry if I've upset you by coming here. Perhaps I should have taken heed of his warnings. After last Monday evening . . . I sort of hoped everything was OK between us now. I certainly had no intention of incurring your wrath again.'

'You haven't.'

'So why not just relax?' he urged, fixing her with a friendly smile. 'Believe it or not, I'm not quite as dreadful as the papers make out. If it is that that's bothering you, you have my word. Exactly like my role of Edwin Crighton in *To Love the Hero*, my intentions are honourable.'

'Honourable?' Rosemary stammered.

'I merely thought as I was in the neighbourhood, and as we got on so well last Monday, it would be nice to have lunch together. There must be a decent pub or restaurant in the area.'

'T-there's quite a good pub in the next village.'

'Good. How long will it take you to get ready?'

'About twenty minutes.'

'Wonderful,' he said, relieved. 'That gives me a chance to move Brian's boxes. I loaded the car so quickly I didn't have time to rearrange the boot.'

'I see Mabel's recovered,' Rosemary remarked, directing Stephen through narrow, winding country lanes to a village green, complete with cricket pitch and ancient wooden pavilion. In the far corner, opposite a row of tiny cottages, stood the village pub. A wealth of old plaster, thatched roof and oak beams, Stephen could only stare in wonderment.

'I thought this kind of place only existed on chocolate boxes, calendars and BBC costume dramas. It's certainly a far cry from my old haunts in Sheffield.'

Lifting the well-used Suffolk latch, Stephen breathed in the comforting yet pungent smell of wood smoke, Brasso and beeswax.

'Oh, I forgot. Mind your head!' Rosemary called, reaching swiftly for his arm. He ducked, just in time. 'Thanks. Tell me, am I unusually tall or is it the locals who are uncommonly small?'

'A bit of both, I should imagine. Years ago a family circus used to have their winter quarters here. You know, midgets and men on stilts.'

Looking about him in the dimly lit room, Stephen saw no sign of either. Instead, propped at the bar were two elderly locals (obviously farm labourers) and in complete contrast, two businessmen in navy pin-striped suits.

'Don't be put off by the lack of customers. It's still early,' Rosemary whispered as an aside, making her way to a table by the fire. 'And the food is exceptionally good. At least it used to be.' She refrained from adding she hadn't eaten here since Gary died.

With Stephen ordering their drinks and food, Rosemary relaxed against the tapestry-backed chair. From here she could study Stephen's strong masculine frame, leaning casually against the bar. Yes, the pub did have a good reputation but she'd also chosen it for its complete lack of direct light. This was far kinder than her own patio doors.

Returning with her red wine and a glass of the local brew, it was Stephen's turn for observation. In her simple mid-calf-length skirt, plain angora sweater and paisley shawl, draped elegantly across her shoulders, he couldn't help but comment.

'You know who you remind me of, sitting there so demurely by the fire, especially with your shawl tucked about your shoulders?'

Rosemary groaned inwardly before responding. 'Your mother?'

'Good heavens, no,' Stephen cried, his subsequent laughter echoing across the bar, causing the locals to turn round and the two businessmen to dislodge their papers. 'Sorry. I didn't mean to embarrass you. I'm forgetting we're not in Sheffield now. No, Rosemary. You're definitely not like my mother. She was almost as tall as me and at least twice your size.'

'Was?'

'She died when I was a lad.'

'I'm so sorry,' Rosemary replied, wondering why those same few words always sounded dreadfully inadequate. 'It must have been a very sad time for you.'

'Aye, it was. Though, it wasn't all bad. Being a TEC with three older sisters, I was at least well taken care of after Mum died.'

'And did they spoil you?'

'Aye. They did that,' Stephen chuckled. 'Especially Mary. Evelyn and Elizabeth weren't quite so easy-going. Still, I expect I deserved a good wallop now and again.'

Trying to think of Stephen as a young boy, Rosemary looked up, faintly bewildered. 'What you said a few moments ago . . . I've heard of the TUC and a great deal of student slang. I'm afraid you've lost me with a TEC. What's that?'

'You mean you've never heard of a Tail End Charlie?'

'Not in that context,' she said as the landlord's wife appeared with portions of home-made steak and ale pie and freshly cooked vegetables.

Leaving the pub after lunch, Stephen nodded appreciatively in the direction of the village green. 'It's certainly very peaceful here, isn't it?'

'Mmm. Particularly in the winter months. Not so in the summer I'm afraid, when the place can be overrun by day-trippers and ice-cream vans. We used to live over there.'

Casting an admiring glance at the impressive properties bordering the common, Stephen said without thinking, 'Is that why you moved?'

'Not exactly. It was more to do with finance after Gary died. Although we were never short of money, shall I just say Gary certainly enjoyed spending it.'

'It must have been very hard leaving such a beautiful spot. Don't you miss it? Or is that too painful a question?'

'It might have been at one time, but not any more,' Rosemary replied, with a cursory glimpse at an impressive-looking house behind wrought-iron gates and sweeping gravel drive. 'Some of my friends thought I was mad leaving, only they weren't fully aware of the circumstances. To be honest, neither was I – then,' she said with a cynical smile. 'Besides it's not so much the house I miss, it's the garden. When the Lupins, Delphiniums and Agapanthus were in flower—'

'Hold on a moment,' Stephen protested, his eyes glinting playfully. 'We might come from the same county but as I've already mentioned, I'm no Geoffrey Smith. Lupins I can just about cope with but as for those things with the virtually unpronounceable names . . . You know, I really do think you should meet my father. You can talk about plants all day. I'm sure you'd like him.'

'Mmm. I think I would. Now, would you like to see the pond?'

'Is that complete with ducks?'

Rosemary shook her head. 'Afraid not. This is a pond of the ancient variety, surrounded by eleven oak trees and supposedly planted by monks many years ago. According to legend they planted one for each disciple.'

Deeply thoughtful, Stephen pushed his hair away from his forehead. 'Hmm. Even though I missed most of our Sunday school sessions, I could have sworn there were twelve disciples.'

The earlier brightness in Rosemary's voice disappeared without trace. 'You're right, there were. But don't you remember? Jesus was betrayed by Judas.'

Something in the tone of her voice caused Stephen to look up. Was she perhaps thinking of her own betrayal, that of her husband and his mistress?

Walking together through the woods, Rosemary forced back dry tears. When the children were small she'd often walked this way with Gary. It had been one of their favourite haunts, particularly when the bluebells were in flower and the hazel buds unfurling. Spotting a squirrel scurry across their path, she gave a melancholy smile.

'Ben was forever trying to catch one, you know, and Jane desperately wanted one for a pet.'

'Really? So what was the outcome?'

'Luckily, Ben was never quick enough to catch one. As far as Jane was concerned I compromised. She had a hamster called Nutkin after the Beatrix Potter character, which was fine until the novelty wore off. That's Jane for you. Now she's even suggesting that I have one of Sarah's puppies.'

'Isn't that your old school-friend with the farm in Wales? The one who encouraged you to write?'

Rosemary nodded, surprised that Stephen should have remembered. 'Anyway, the puppy is a definite no-no, even if they weren't all spoken for. My house and garden are much too small.'

For the next five minutes the two of them walked in silence along the twisting woodland path, Stephen thinking how different all this was compared to the Sheffield streets of his childhood and Rosemary letting her fingers trail against familiar gnarled tree trunks and clumps of coppiced hazel. Already in her mind's eye were two small figures. Warmly clad, wearing brightly striped bobble hats and shiny red wellingtons, they kicked their way through endless drifts of fallen leaves.

As if reading her mind, Stephen placed a comforting arm about her shoulders.

'You miss them, don't you?'

'Yes. I suppose I do,' Rosemary acknowledged, a solitary tear glinting on her cheek. 'But at almost nineteen and twenty-one, they have their own lives to lead now. It would be selfish of me to hold them back. Still, I am hoping to see

Jane soon. Oliver said I can take her to rehearsals. I'm also planning to see Ben during the next couple of weeks.'

'Then why don't I give you a lift?' Stephen suggested, his arm still on her shoulders. 'I've already arranged to see my dad the week after next. Didn't you say you don't like driving in Sheffield? Why not give Ben a ring when we get back?'

'If you're sure Mabel won't mind?' Rosemary said shyly.

'We'd both be glad of your company. Meanwhile, where's this pond you mentioned earlier? Or were you simply pulling my leg?'

When Stephen slipped his arm through hers, Rosemary made no attempt to pull away. There was no need. Unlike this morning when he first arrived, she now felt perfectly at ease in his company. Welcoming his very presence and the closeness of his body, they walked arm in arm to the pond.

Chapter 7

Dialling Ben's number, Rosemary hoped and prayed he would be in his room. She knew the phone was on the ground floor and someone was usually in halls. When a girl's voice answered it wasn't long before Ben was summoned to the phone.

Anxious to tell her son of Stephen's offer of a lift to Sheffield, Rosemary was disappointed with the response. Moments later she returned to the lounge.

'It wasn't a very good line, I'm afraid. From what I could make out Ben's busy that day. He mentioned something about going to The Blades. Funny really, I can't imagine Ben ice-skating.'

Stephen smiled broadly. 'Rosemary, you obviously know a great deal about gardening but not much about football. The Blades are the local football team – Sheffield United.'

Registering Rosemary's blushes, Stephen continued, 'Anyway, good for Ben. Shows he's really settled into Sheffield life if he's a Blades supporter. Dad and I have a season ticket. Wait a minute! Perhaps you should see The Blades in action for yourself. Ring Ben back. Tell him I'll arrange tickets for all of us. You can see him before lunch; I can catch up with my dad and we'll all meet up for the match. How does that sound?'

Initially unsure with what he was proposing, Rosemary was soon persuaded to ring Ben again. This time she was delighted with his response.

Finalizing arrangements, Stephen looked at his watch. 'Looks like time's caught up with me. I'd better dash if I'm going to catch Brian at Swallow Park.'

'Would you like to ring – let him know you're on your way?'

'No, thanks. If he's not there I'll simply leave everything with security.'

Walking with him to his car, Rosemary thanked Stephen for lunch and also for bringing the photos.

'Not at all. It's me who should be thanking you for coffee and the guided tour. I hope they never chop down those amazing trees.'

Pausing by the car door and much to her surprise, Stephen bent and kissed her cheek. 'Bye, Rosemary. It's been a lovely day. Take care and don't forget to wrap up warm for the match. See you soon.' With that he climbed into Mabel, switched on the ignition and with a wave of the hand was gone.

Watching him reverse the car down the drive, Rosemary raised her own hand to her cheek. Saturday week couldn't come quickly enough. Before that, however, she must ring Jane. What did women her age wear to football matches?

'Jane, darling?'

'Mum? What's wrong? You never ring at this time.'

'Oh, I was ... um ... wondering if you could advise me what I should wear to a proper football match?'

'What you always wear, I suppose. Anyway, what exactly

do you mean by "a proper football match"? Don't tell me you've been roped in by Mr Webster to support Ben's old team in the inter-schools tournament?'

'No. I'm going to Sheffield to see The Blades and—'

'Crikey! I didn't think you were that keen on football. When Ben left for uni you said how pleased you were not to be ferrying him to football each Saturday.'

'Well, yes . . . Only this time it's different. It's sort of *special*.'

Special? Jane frowned. As far as she and her mother were concerned, football had never been *special*.

As if reading her daughter's mind, Rosemary attempted nonchalance. She wasn't very successful. 'Special as in . . . Stephen Walker's invited me.'

A squeal of disbelief echoed down the line. 'What? You and . . . I thought you said he was rude and arrogant.'

'Perhaps I made a mistake. So will you please hurry up and tell me what to wear. Having just received the phone bill you and Ben ran up at Christmas I'd like to keep this conversation brief.'

'OK,' Jane agreed, anxious not to be reminded of bills. Nevertheless she was still slightly put out. She'd been hoping for a full-blown account as to why Stephen Walker should suddenly be inviting her mother to a football match. 'You're obviously going to need trousers and something warm. Bootlegs, combat trousers or jeans, plus a thick sweater or fleece. It can be jolly cold on the terraces.'

'But I've only got my old gardening trousers and I couldn't possibly wear jeans. They'd make me look enormous. Remember what your father used to say about my thighs?'

'Oh, Mum. You're impossible. There's absolutely nothing wrong with your thighs. Gracious, you're far slimmer than me. If you want my opinion, and not wishing to open up old wounds, I reckon Dad deliberately bought you unflattering clothes and made such derisive comments because he was afraid of you going off with someone else.'

'I was *never* unfaithful to your father.'

'Precisely. Because it would have ruined his little set-up if you were. Anyway, like I said, don't let's bring that up again. Just make sure you buy yourself something really super for sexy Stephen. I bet he adores women with shapely thighs. Gosh. I can't wait to tell Rebecca and the gang. My mother and Stephen Walker. Wow!'

'Jane,' Rosemary protested. 'It's not like that at all. I'm only going because . . .'

'Sorry, Mum. No time. I'm late as it is. I have to see my tutor about my dissertation. Besides, didn't you say you were worried about the phone bill? *Ciao*. Oh, by the way—'

Hanging up the phone, Rosemary conjured up a mental picture of herself wearing combat trousers. Ben would never forgive her. And what was it Jane had instructed before dashing off? *'Wear something red and black. It's S.U.'s colours.'* Thankfully, she already possessed a short black jacket and it shouldn't be too difficult to find a red sweater.

Fuelled by a sense of both guilt and satisfaction, Stephen headed south past brightly painted hoardings. Ignoring the signs, advertising vacant units at Swallow Park, he turned sharply in the direction of London and the motorway.

'Phew. That was close,' he muttered to himself, conscious of the empty film boxes sliding across the back seat of the car and colliding in Mabel's boot. Thank goodness they hadn't done that when they'd driven to the pub for lunch.

Stephen sucked his cheeks reflectively. At least part of his story was true. The boxes were indeed for a Brian but not a

Brian at Swallow Park. He didn't know anyone at Swallow Park or even that it existed until today. It had all been part of an elaborate plot to see Rosemary again.

Discovering that he wasn't needed at the studio and that Oliver was planning to send Rosemary some photos, Stephen saw it as a heaven-sent opportunity. In addition to this, Brian (Oliver's director of photography) was also moving house. Offering to drop the empty boxes off at Brian's flat – so his partner could begin packing – Stephen had the perfect alibi. The only problem being, he deduced, heading north, was how to make the whole performance convincing. Passing Swallow Park had been the inspiration he'd been searching for without arousing suspicion.

Remembering the look on Rosemary's face when he'd kissed her goodbye, Stephen smiled indulgently and nosed Mabel towards the slip road of the M1. Yes, fortunately for him events leading up to that moment had been part of a pretty convincing performance. All in all it had been quite a remarkable day and he'd enjoyed Rosemary's company immensely. Now all he had to do was find Brian's flatmate.

The day before the match Rosemary arrived at Curl Up and Dye for an appointment with Vickie. Wearing her hair short meant it was now far easier to manage, yet she still wanted it to look right for her very special day. All the stylists, she noticed, regardless of size, were wearing bright pink tops and black bootleg trousers.

'They're so comfortable, Mrs Fielding,' Vickie said, when Rosemary passed comment. 'Especially when they're well cut, like these. There's loads in the shop across the way – and there's a sale on. Why not take a look?'

Not entirely convinced, Rosemary crossed the road. Spying

the aforementioned establishment, she hesitated with one hand on the door. What on earth was it – clothes shop, jungle or zoo?

'Oh, well, needs must, I suppose,' Rosemary muttered grimly, entering what one of her heroines would have described as dubious portals.

Greeted by an ear-splitting cacophony of jungle drums and pipes, Rosemary waited until her eyes became gradually accustomed to the flashing lights. In time she discerned a collection of circular clothes rails, each with an artificial palm tree sprouting forth from the centre. She gave an involuntary shudder. What was she doing here? It was certainly a far cry from her usual shopping haunts and the elegant displays of Regent Street.

Dangling below a garish *50% OFF* sale board were numerous pairs of once fashionable, multi-coloured leggings. Their waists stretched to bursting point, they hung like skinned animals on a gibbet. Likening the assorted patterns to a jungle full of animals, Rosemary concluded the World Wildlife Fund would have a field day, were it not for the fact that these animal pelts were made of spandex, lycra and jersey.

'I know they ain't fashionable any more but they ain't 'alf comfortable,' came a voice from a swirl of plastic lianas, stuffed parrots and imitation fruit.

Rosemary gaped, astonished. So busy telling herself that she'd never be seen dead in something resembling a giraffe or a zebra, she hadn't noticed the young sales assistant heading towards her.

'I think we've got a few plain ones left as well,' the ghostly white face continued, nodding to a far corner. 'What size are yer?'

Trying her best to ignore the multi-pierced ears, nose and

eyebrows, Rosemary smiled graciously. 'Actually, I was, er, looking for some bootleg trousers. Vickie from the hairdressers said . . .'

At the mention of Vickie's name, Rosemary was directed first to the appropriate clothes rail and later to the communal changing room. To her horror she discovered she was not alone. Two embarrassed schoolgirls stood huddled in a corner with a selection of the aforementioned cut-price leggings.

'We want 'em for a fancy dress party,' said one, struggling into a skinned giraffe.

'Yeah,' replied the other. 'It's gonna be an oldies evenin'. Yer know. Glam rock, shell suits and leggin's.'

Rosemary cringed inwardly at the word 'oldies'. No doubt the newly clad zebra and giraffe would be wondering what this particular oldie was doing here. Disentangling a pair of bootleg trousers from a jagged-toothed hanger, she ventured nervously in the direction of the mirror.

'Cor. They look really good on 'er, don't they?' said the giraffe.

'Yeah. They do. I wish my mum would wear 'em but she's so bleedin' old-fashioned,' announced the zebra. 'Are you gonna 'av 'em?'

Twenty minutes later Rosemary found herself emerging reasonably unscathed from the jungle with not only a pair of black bootleg trousers but also a pair of fine leather ankle boots. She'd opted for the latter in preference to Doc Martens, as suggested by her animal companions. Her intention was to watch the game of football, *not* take part in it.

On the morning of the match, Stephen arrived early, their arrangement being that Rosemary was to have lunch with

Ben, followed by some shopping, and then meet Stephen outside the gates of Bramhall Lane. Before that Stephen was planning to see his father. He asked Rosemary if she would care to join him.

'I must warn you he's extremely wary of southerners and also acutely aware of the north-south divide,' Stephen explained, with a tinge of embarrassment. 'There was a great deal of resentment in the area once the steel works closed down and the men were laid off. I shan't be offended if you don't want to risk it.'

Bemused by the word 'risk', Rosemary decided to go. Wouldn't it be nice to meet a member of Stephen's family? Particularly as she knew so little about his early life. Once they neared the allotment, however, her nervousness began to show.

'Don't worry,' Stephen assured her. 'I'm convinced the two of you will hit it off immediately. People say we're very much alike.'

Reminded of her earlier meetings with Stephen, this comment did absolutely nothing to allay Rosemary's fears. Could Mr Walker senior be even worse?

Reading her mind, Stephen placed a guiding hand on her elbow and fixed her with another of his disarming smiles. 'We're really not too bad when you get to know us – honestly.'

She would have recognized Stephen's father instantly, such was the likeness between father and son. The once dark blond hair was still thick like Stephen's and he possessed the same proud jawline and brow. The only marked difference was in stature, Rosemary noted. Ted Walker's once upright frame, now slightly stooped, belied his seventy-plus years. Watching him carefully, she also perceived he was in the middle of clearing his plot for spring sowing.

'Stephen, lad!' The old man's face shone radiant at the sight of his son, yet froze almost immediately when he saw Rosemary by his side.

'Dad. I'd like you to meet Rosemary Fielding, better known perhaps as Romy Felden. She's an author and wrote the production I'm involved with at the moment.'

Muttering something under his breath about fancy names and what was wrong with the one you were born with, Ted Walker announced abruptly, 'How do you do, Miss Felden. I won't shake your hand. I'm all mucky from bonfire and compost.'

The tone was cold and unwelcoming, leaving Rosemary to feel like an intruder. As far as she could tell, Ted Walker's hands appeared perfectly clean. Sensing an air of distinct hostility, she left Stephen's side and wandered off to look round the allotment.

Ten minutes later, having examined weed-free seed drills and newly erected broad bean cloches, she noticed father and son still deep in conversation. Stephen looked up and smiled as she passed. Ted said nothing. He merely fixed her with a flinty glare.

Brushing aside the distinct feeling of unease, Rosemary pushed her hands deep into the pockets of her jacket and peered into the window of the potting shed. Just as she'd suspected from the nearby, neatly dug trenches, Ted Walker's shed was home to assorted varieties of potato tubers. All laid in rows with military precision (their purple eyes uppermost), they stood erect against a backdrop of brightly coloured seed packets.

Without warning Rosemary felt a lump in her throat, the familiar sight and smell of it all prompting nostalgia for her old garden. Willing herself not to cry, she turned to find

Stephen and his father regarding her closely.

'Stephen tells me you're interested in gardening, Miss Felden. Is that right?'

Sensing a less hostile tone, Rosemary found herself drawn into a conversation on root crops, clay soil and problems with new gardens. Recognizing the familiar words, peas, beans and carrots, Stephen pursed his lips in understanding, only to cry out in confusion when Rosemary started on the subject of Brassicas.

'Hey, hold on a minute. All this *Gardeners' World* stuff is getting beyond me. I haven't a clue what you're talking about.'

Ted Walker grinned and lit his pipe. 'Aye, lad. You've never been one for gardening, have you?'

'No,' came the reply. 'For the moment I prefer to leave that to you and Rosemary.'

'Unfortunately, I no longer have the time or the space for vegetables,' Rosemary explained.

Puzzled, Ted scratched his head and removed his pipe. Hadn't Stephen said she was a writer? 'Nay, lass, 'appen you don't,' he concluded.

Stephen looked at his watch. 'I suppose we'd better be going. Can we give you a lift home, Dad?'

The old man declined, nodding in the direction of his bike. 'That's all the transport I need, lad. You can tell Mary I'm on my way.'

'I'll call for you later, then?'

'Aye. Goodbye, Miss, er, Felden. Nice to have met you,' Ted said softly, with a kindly light in his eye and even extending his hand in greeting.

Convinced that he'd winked at her, Rosemary was completely taken aback when she heard him say. 'Why not get

Stephen to bring you again to check on the Brassicas?'

'Will he be coming to the match too?' Rosemary asked as they walked away.

'No, he's decided against it today, said he'd rather watch it on TV. In the meantime, while you have lunch with Ben, I shall be taking him to the cemetery to visit my mother's grave. I confess I forgot. It would have been their wedding anniversary today.'

'Then we can't possibly go to the match.'

'Course we can. Mother wouldn't have wanted us to be miserable. She wasn't that type of person. Come along,' he said, opening Mabel's passenger door. 'There's something else I want to show you.'

In reflective silence, Stephen drove through street after street of derelict buildings, the walls covered in graffiti and the windows smashed and broken. At length, slowing down outside what had once been a proud monument to the steel industry, he announced quietly, 'That's where I used to work.'

Visibly shocked to think of his strong, lean frame and fine hands working in the sweat and heat of the foundry, Rosemary felt it inappropriate to comment. Stephen and his father had every right to feel embittered and angry.

Moving on again, their journey continued through narrow streets of terraced houses. These, just like the factories, were also derelict and boarded up.

'They're due for demolition,' Stephen said huskily.

Turning away from the shattered, cobweb-streaked windows and broken gutters, Rosemary studied Stephen's face. His earlier bright countenance now bore a distinct shade of grey, as if reflecting the sombre, shadowy surroundings.

Saying nothing, Stephen's thoughts drifted back to his childhood. A time when groups of innocent and carefree children played in the streets, their shouts and laughter echoing above the noise of the nearby foundry. Watched over by mothers in brightly patterned aprons, steps were scrubbed, windows were polished and freshly laundered washing strung on high. What mattered about the tell-tale smuts from the factories, their menfolk argued, at least it was evidence of work and wages. Now it was nothing but distant memories and decay.

Suddenly reminded of Rosemary's presence, Stephen pointed to the bottom of the street. 'Our house was fourth from the end. My friend Tony lived opposite.' His jaw set hard when he regarded the blackened shell of the building.

'What happened?' she asked, almost dreading his reply.

'The whole family perished in a fire. Tony's father had been laid off. With no money for electricity, they used candles . . .'

Rosemary's voice caught in her throat. 'Oh, Stephen, I'm so sorry.'

'And I'm sorry too. I should never have brought you here. I just hoped it might help you understand.'

'There's no need to apologize,' she said, blinking back tears and reaching for his hand. 'Of course I understand. In fact I understand perfectly.'

Before dropping Rosemary off at the Botanical Gardens, where she'd arranged to meet Ben, Stephen insisted they call at his sister's for a quick coffee. To her surprise, Mary, the youngest of his three sisters, proved to be older than herself. Married with two sons and already a grandmother, Mary explained that Ted Walker had reluctantly moved in with them when Stephen left Sheffield, only on the condition that he could keep his allotment.

Living in a large three-storey house on the Eccleshall Road, there was plenty of space for everyone. Rosemary delighted in its bright and shiny appearance. With the smell of lavender polish reminding her of Freda and Norfolk, it was strangely comforting to think of Ted Walker living in such pleasant surroundings.

'Frank's taken the grandchildren swimming,' Mary said, bringing in a tray of coffee and biscuits. 'Don't worry, they'll be back in good time for the match. Thanks for the tickets Stephen. You spoil them, you know. I'm not surprised they think the world of you.'

Acutely embarrassed, Stephen changed the subject. 'By the way, Dad says he'll be back shortly and I've already collected the flowers he wanted for Mum's grave. Is he keeping all right, do you think? He had me right worried after that last bout of flu.'

Passing Stephen the plate of biscuits, Mary replied, 'He certainly seems better but I do wish he'd give up riding that old bike of his. Then again, he's like you – stubborn and won't give in.' She smiled, giving Rosemary a knowing look.

Deciding that she liked Stephen's sister, Rosemary was equally pleased to discover *To Love the Hero* was one of Mary's favourite books. It had been a Christmas present from one of the grandchildren.

'Why don't you ask Rosemary to autograph it for you?' Stephen suggested.

'I'll do better than that,' Rosemary replied, when Mary returned with her well-thumbed paperback. 'I'll also send you a hard-cover edition when I get home. After all, it seems only right if your brother is playing the part of my hero.'

Sitting at the table thinking of a suitable inscription,

Rosemary failed to notice Mary's self-satisfied grin which appeared to be saying, '*Miss Felden, knowing my brother as I do, this time he's definitely not playing!*'

Chapter 8

Waiting by the botanical gardens, Rosemary played with the collar on her jacket. It had been several weeks since she'd seen her son, who as yet wasn't aware of her new hairstyle.

'Mum? What have you done to yourself?' Ben called, bounding down the steps. 'Your hair looks wicked.'

Reminding herself this was a compliment, Rosemary was secretly delighted when Ben nodded approvingly at her black bootleg trousers, jacket and red polo neck sweater. They had already drawn admiring comments from Stephen when he'd first arrived to collect her.

After lunch and a record-breaking shopping trip for jeans and trainers, mother and son made their way to Bramhall Lane, Rosemary registering the cost of the newly purchased hovercraft welded to Ben's feet and he in turn puzzling why his mother was so nervous about going to a football match.

Watching crowds surge in droves towards the gates, Rosemary became increasingly anxious. This was hardly the inter-schools championship. So many people. All the jostling and noise. What if Stephen was held up? Worse still, what if he couldn't find her? Even Ben was beginning to show familiar signs of agitation as kick-off time drew near.

Taken completely by surprise, she saw him above a group of bobbing heads. Stephen, fair hair falling across his face as he ran, smiled and waved.

'Sorry to keep you waiting,' he gasped breathlessly. 'Wouldn't you just know it. I had problems with Mabel. As for parking . . .'

'Stephen's car,' Rosemary explained in response to Ben's raised eyebrows, and introduced her son.

With the trio hurrying towards the turnstiles, Stephen held a carrier bag in Rosemary's direction. This is for you, to add to your collection. The perfect finishing touch.' Stephen beamed, watching her peer into the bag and pull out a long red and white scarf. Taking it from her hand, he wound it carefully around her throat and shoulders. 'Now you're a true Blades supporter.'

Thanking him for his gift, her attention diverted by a bois-terous crowd of latecomers, Rosemary felt herself propelled into Stephen's arms. Pushed and shoved from behind, he held her protectively while Ben looked on, mildly curious. His mother a Blades supporter? Asked this question six months ago, he would have said never in a million years. Now, he had to admit that attired in red, white and black, she certainly looked convincing.

Trying to remember the key players in both teams, Rosemary was soon caught up in the resulting euphoria when The Blades scored the opening goal. Amidst a sea of cheering red and white, Stephen and Ben exchanged hurried comments on tactics and team placings. By half-time, however, their animated conversation gave way to gloom and despondency. The opposition had equalized.

With endless corners and penalties, the atmosphere became ever more tense. Ben looked at his watch. Only three minutes to go. Rosemary in turn studied Stephen's troubled face. For her sake, he'd so wanted his team to win.

Her attention momentarily off the pitch, Rosemary was taken completely off guard when red and white banners filled the stadium. The Sheffield crowd erupted into loud and ecstatic cheers; Ben was euphoric and Stephen hugged her, lifting her high in the air, the sheer pleasure on their faces a joy to behold. Whatever happened after the match, she told herself, she must never confess to missing the winning goal.

'We'd better leave quickly,' Stephen urged. 'In case there's any trouble from the opposition.' Grabbing her hand and calling over his shoulder to Ben, he led the way to safety.

'So, what's it to be Ben? Burgers, Italian or Greek?'

Listening to Stephen reel off a list of familiar eating places, Rosemary secretly yearned for a moussaka – it was hungry work supporting your team. In recent weeks she'd already eaten Italian three times. Twice with Jane and Ben and then again on her never to be forgotten dinner date with Stephen. Her heart sank; Ben had already decided on a nearby burger bar.

'Don't worry,' Stephen whispered as an aside, as if sensing her disappointment. 'Perhaps you and I can get together for a quiet meal, later in the week?'

Warmed by the prospect of such a meeting (she'd have so much to tell Sarah when she called), Rosemary caught sight of her reflection in a shop window. It wasn't only her life that had changed, it was her whole appearance. What was it they said about women wanting to find themselves? Unlike Meryl Streep in the film *Kramer vs. Kramer*, she hadn't deliberately set out to *find herself* but she was certainly enjoying this new-found relaxed attitude to life.

With Stephen at the counter seeing to their order, Ben unzipped his jacket and turned to his mother. 'He's great, Mum. Not at all how I'd imagined. I'll admit the hair was a bit of a shock – his, not yours – but I guess it suits the role he's playing.'

Slowly unwinding the scarf from her neck, Rosemary nodded in agreement. It wasn't only Stephen's hair that suited the role, it was everything about him. With her train of thought chugging past, she paused to recall a conversation she'd had with Sarah, several years ago. At the time they'd been watching Stephen in a TV costume drama and also sharing a bottle of wine.

'Just look at that body, Ro,' Sarah had giggled, somewhat the worse for wear. 'Go on, admit it. Wouldn't you just like to get your hands on that?'

At the time Rosemary had replied in the negative. As well as courting a string of brainless bimbos, Stephen had also courted some extremely unpleasant publicity. Today, faced with the same question and knowing you couldn't believe everything you read in the papers, she would have replied in a different vein. The very thought of getting her hands on Stephen brought a flood of colour to her cheeks.

Clever as he was, Ben couldn't read his mother's thoughts and fortunately for Rosemary his attention was elsewhere – Stephen and his approaching meal.

'Are you all right, Rosemary? You look a bit flushed. It is rather warm in here. Can I help you with your jacket?'

Rosemary blinked, willing herself to concentrate on undoing her buttons before passing it to Stephen to hook on the back of her chair. Grateful for the diversion, she disentangled assorted cardboard and polystyrene wrappers and ate her meal in silence. Perhaps in the circumstances it was safer to leave conversation to Ben and Stephen.

'Yes. We'll have to do that next,' Stephen agreed, when talk progressed from football to another contact sport. 'How about it, Rosemary? Ice hockey?'

'Ice hockey? I'm only just getting used to professional football.'

'Oh, you'll soon pick it up, Mum. You have three periods of play instead of two, and five players who are constantly changing. Of course the penalties are completely different but—'

'Ben. Stop. I'm already completely confused.'

Dropping Ben outside his halls of residence, Stephen shook him warmly by the hand. 'I'll try and get some ice hockey tickets if you like. And what about the Cup Final? Would you be interested?'

Interested? Ben grinned from ear to ear. He'd never been to Wembley. Needless to say, his father had always promised to take him. Somehow or other, one of Gary's unexpected business trips invariably cropped up at the very last minute.

By the time Stephen pointed Mabel in the direction of the motorway, he was looking distinctly tired.

'Perhaps we should stop for a coffee?' Rosemary suggested, concerned that he might fall asleep at the wheel. 'If you like I can even share some of the driving. That's if Mabel will allow it?'

'Coffee sounds like a good idea,' Stephen said, pulling into the next service station. 'Although, I'm not so sure about Mabel. Like most women, she can be a bit temperamental at times.'

Rosemary dug him playfully in the ribs. 'Cheek! And there was me concerned for your welfare.'

Without warning, Stephen gave a mock bow, reached for her hand and drew it to his lips. 'I'm extremely grateful for your concern, ma'am. By the way, my father likes you.'

'What makes you say that?'

'For a start, he told me. It must have been the gardening bit that did it. Incidentally, what are Brassicas? Sounds like a form of medieval underwear to me.'

Admonishing him playfully for his ignorance, she teased, 'That explains why you haven't got curly hair. You never ate your Brassicas when you were a little boy.'

By the time Mabel heaved and groaned into Rosemary's drive, the effects of service-station coffee had already long worn off. It wasn't only Mabel who was suffering from chronic fatigue.

'Stephen, why didn't you tell me you'd been at the studio half the night? If Oliver wants you for an early shoot tomorrow, you're going to be absolutely exhausted. You can't possibly drive any further tonight.'

Too tired to argue, Stephen yawned and shrugged his shoulders as if in defeat.

'Why don't you stay?' Rosemary ventured nervously. 'The spare room-cum-study's a bit of a mess at the moment, but I always keep Ben's bed made up.'

Needing little persuasion, Stephen stepped from the car. Despite his tiredness, Rosemary's suggested sleeping arrangement had registered perfectly. With mixed emotions he followed her upstairs. Perhaps in the present circumstances it was all for the best.

'I'm afraid it is rather, er, unusual in here,' she explained, opening the door to Ben's room. 'I only hope you don't have nightmares.'

Stephen surveyed the room with its black ceiling, two red

walls and two white. On the red walls hung a bass guitar, posters of heavy metal bands and football teams, while on the white hung maps and photos of assorted geographical features.

He gave a wry smile. 'I might not know any of the groups – a sure sign of growing old – but I'd be a disgrace to my county if I didn't recognize those photographs of Malham Cove, Malham Tarn and that familiar limestone pavement.'

'I understand it's a favourite haunt of A level students,' Rosemary said, taking a pair of blue pyjamas from a drawer. 'These are brand new. Ben refuses to wear them. He tells me it's all boxer shorts these days.'

Placing the pyjamas on the bed, Rosemary fetched Stephen a towel and pointed to the bathroom. 'There's plenty of hot water if you want a bath or shower. Don't worry. You won't disturb me. I have my own en suite, albeit small. Believe me, it's a godsend when sharing the house with two teenagers. Now, if you're really sure you don't want anything else to eat or drink . . .'

As she turned to go, Stephen gathered her gently into his arms. Their lips met briefly. 'Rosemary, I think . . .'

'And I think you're exhausted,' she whispered, breaking away. 'You also need a decent night's sleep.'

'Yes . . . I think perhaps I do.'

Standing on tiptoe, Rosemary kissed him lightly on the cheek. 'The joys of being an actor. Sleep well and I'll give you a call in the morning.'

'There's no need. I shall have to be up at the crack of sparrow, as they say.'

'Even so, you'll need breakfast. Oliver can't expect you to work on an empty stomach.'

For a while, as she lay in bed, Rosemary's thoughts turned

to Stephen in the very next room. Separated by only a partition wall, she found herself wondering what he'd been going to say. Would things have been any different if he hadn't been so tired? He did appear to be enjoying her company but wasn't she forgetting two important facts? To begin with, she was seven years older, and secondly, she was also the mother of two grown-up children.

Grown up? Rosemary gave a reflective smile in the darkness. Despite their ages, there were times when she could hardly class Ben and Jane as grown up. Serious debates (concerning family matters, university issues and current affairs) apart, there was the odd occasion when they still behaved like children. While we're on the subject of children, she told herself, aren't you also behaving rather childishly?

Her mind a jumble of thoughts, Rosemary eventually drifted into a deep and dreamless sleep. So deep, in fact, she never heard Stephen leave. Fully expecting to prepare him some breakfast, all she found was his note on the kitchen table.

'*4.30a.m. Couldn't possibly disturb you. Thanks for the bed. Sorry I was so tired. Will call you. Stephen.*'

Clutching the note against her breast, she hurried to Ben's room for any sign of the previous night's occupant. To her dismay there was none. The pyjamas lay untouched (presumably unworn) and everything was just as before. Rosemary was devastated. Surely there must be something. Reminding herself he'd arrived with nothing, so was unlikely to have left anything behind, she sat on the foot of the bed and re-read his hastily written message.

Eventually, turning her gaze to the posters of Malham, she thought how wonderful it would be to walk there with Stephen. The wind in their faces, their arms linked together . . .

She sighed, longingly. This was no good. *No* good at all. To begin with she was here in Ben's bedroom and Stephen no doubt was miles away and well into the day's filming. There was nothing for it but to strip the bed ready for Ben's next visit at Easter and keep herself busy for the rest of the day.

Throwing back the duvet, her heart soared. In the pillow was the merest indentation where Stephen's head had lain. Caressing the faint hollow she remembered his simple message. Although he'd written that he'd call her, would he be true to his word?

That night before going to bed, Rosemary opened the drawer of her dressing-table. Reaching in, she placed the well-thumbed and well-read message next to his rose.

In the week that followed, Stephen rang only once, saying he couldn't make dinner as previously planned. Countless members of cast and crew had gone down with flu. Filming was in chaos and for once Oliver was shooting out of sequence – something the usually quiet American truly loathed.

'Oliver is not a happy man,' Stephen explained. 'Is there any chance of you coming to the studio instead? If so, why not bring Jane?'

Delighted to hear from her mother, Jane put revision on hold. The lure of seeing Fergus Buchanan on set, and the possibility that he might actually speak to her, was all too much. She was ecstatic.

'I gather you enjoyed the football.'

'Yes. Who told you?'

'Ben.'

'You always say Ben never rings,' Rosemary exclaimed in disbelief.

'Ah-ha, well, this time he did. Not only did he give me a blow-by-blow account of the match, but also he described what you were wearing – can you believe that? *And* he told me all about the dishy man you were with.'

'Jane. You honestly don't expect me to believe Ben called Stephen *dishy*?'

'No. Not exactly. But he did say he thought he was ace. In my book that means dishy. In Ben's I should imagine that means he and Stephen got on well together.'

'Yes . . . come to think of it, they did.'

'And hostilities are definitely a thing of the past. You're no longer at each other's throats?'

'You could say that,' Rosemary replied, reminded of last Saturday. They hadn't been at each other's throats but would they have been at anything else if Stephen hadn't been quite so tired? Blushing at the very thought, Rosemary added hurriedly, 'Shall I come to the flat or will you meet me at the station?'

'I'll meet you at Euston. We can go straight to the studio from there. By the way, I can't wait to see your hair.'

As promised, Jane was waiting by the ticket barrier.

'Gosh, Mum, just look at you. You look simply gorgeous. You know, if Ben hadn't warned me I doubt if I'd have recognized you.'

'I haven't changed that much, surely?' Rosemary said, hugging her daughter warmly. 'And was that both a compliment and a sign of approval?'

'Approval? You bet. It suits you. Why haven't you worn your hair that short before?'

'Because your father always preferred it longer. Every time I suggested having it cut he . . . well, you know?'

With a protective gesture, Jane took hold of her mother's arm. 'From now on, you do exactly what you want. OK?'

Something in Jane's tone told Rosemary this statement could be interpreted in many ways. Was she waiting for a response?

'Mum?'

'Yes?'

'You do understand what I'm getting at, don't you?'

'I . . . um . . . think so.'

'Good. I'm glad we've got that sorted. Now, all you have to do is lead me straight to the arms of Fergus Buchanan so I can lust after his gorgeous body.'

Unfortunately for Jane and unbeknown to Rosemary, Oliver had already marked that day for something less gorgeous. Jane was mortified. Obscured in the shadows where she sat with her mother, she sobbed uncontrollably watching Fergus die. There were tears on Rosemary's cheeks too but not for the same reason. Unlike her daughter, Rosemary only had eyes for Stephen. In his role of Edwin Crighton (the compassionate hero), he was at this very moment sweeping the very young and exceptionally pretty Rachel Masters into his arms.

Rosemary closed her eyes, thankful she had written a gentle Regency romance and not a so-called bodice ripper, where everyone hopped into bed naked. In *To Love the Hero* most of her characters behaved with the utmost modesty and decorum. Mercifully, Oliver had ignored Seth Usher's deviation from the original plot, choosing instead to keep to her chosen storyline.

With the final take completed, Stephen walked towards them. Seeing him dressed in stylish silk breeches and tailored morning coat, Rosemary's stomach gave the now-familiar lurch. Jane, meanwhile, reached for yet another tissue and turned red-rimmed eyes in their direction, ignoring Stephen completely.

'Oh, Mum. How could you?'

'Don't take it personally, Stephen,' Rosemary explained. 'Jane says she'll never forgive me for killing off Fergus.'

'Really? How dreadful,' he chuckled. 'Not even if you go and introduce her? Because at this very moment Fergus appears to be making quite a remarkable recovery. Why not take your distraught daughter to meet her idol? Rest assured, as he's just died, Oliver will have no further need of him.'

For once tongue-tied and deeply overawed, Jane clung to her mother's arm as they crossed the studio floor.

'Make sure you come straight back,' Stephen urged softly.

Leaving Jane in her element, Rosemary returned to his side.

'I've missed you,' he said in a hushed tone, taking her hand and leading her to a quiet corner. 'I'm also truly sorry I never got a chance to say goodbye. It didn't seem fair to wake you and I wanted so much to . . .'

There was no time for Stephen to finish his sentence. Oliver was calling. Fergus might be dead and therefore free to be swooned over by Jane; Stephen on the other hand was very much alive.

He emitted an exasperated sigh. 'Sorry, I shall have to go. Oliver's been like a bear with a sore head since this flu epidemic. Perhaps we can meet later? How long are you staying over?'

Rosemary shook her head. 'I'm afraid I hadn't planned to. And with Oliver in his current mood it's probably not a good idea.'

'You're not staying with Jane?'

'Not this time. The flat's only small and her finals are looming. The last thing she needs is her mother lumbering the place up.'

'You're welcome to lumber up my place – if you like?'

Unsure as to whether or not Stephen was being serious or merely joking, she never got to find out. Oliver's irate voice echoed across the set, causing everyone to look in their direction.

'Stephen! Will you please get your ass over here!'

'You'd better go,' Rosemary insisted. 'Otherwise he'll be asking me to write an extra death scene. Look, Easter will soon be here and I'm sure Oliver mentioned returning to the States to see Miriam and the rest of his family. Give me a ring if you're free. Perhaps come and have supper with us, that's if you're up to it? However, I feel it's only fair to warn you, with Ben and Jane home for revision the atmosphere could be extremely tense.

'No worse than here,' he muttered, planting a kiss on her cheek.

'I think we'd better go,' Rosemary hissed, leading Jane away.

'Oh, do we have to? Fergus was just saying . . .'

'Fergus will have to wait, I'm afraid. For the moment I don't think we should outstay our welcome. Besides, I promise to make it up to you in another way.'

'You couldn't possibly,' Jane sniffed.

'Couldn't I? What a pity. And there was me thinking you also wanted to meet Jake De Havilland. As he just happens to be Stephen's best friend and ex-flat-mate . . .'

'Mum!' Jane shrieked, before feeling her mother's hand clamped across her mouth, and she found herself literally dragged from the studio.

Chapter 9

During the Easter vacation the house was in turmoil. Pressure of looming exams resulted in one of two mental states. Euphoria when things went well. Abject doom when they didn't. Rosemary wasn't quite sure which she preferred. The first resulted in endless high spirits and harmless teasing between brother and sister. The latter reduced them to the slough of despair. On such days even the house, painted in an array of pale cream, peach and apricot tints (as if to compensate for the sadly missed walled garden and orchard) radiated an air of gloom.

Rosemary peered across the breakfast table, unsure if today was to be a high or a low.

'When are you going to the studio again?' Ben mumbled through a slice of toast and Marmite.

'I'm not sure. I think it's mostly location work from now on.'

Jane appeared in the doorway, fresh from the shower. She towelled her long wet hair. 'What about Stephen? When are you seeing him again? Only I wanted to ask him about the new Radclyffe play. Did you know his friend has the leading role?'

Ben yawned noisily. 'If you mean that chap with the stupid name. Yes. You've told us a hundred times already.'

'Stupid name. What stupid name?'

'That Jake Boeing fellow.'

'It's Jake De Havilland, idiot! It's not a stupid name at all,' Jane snorted, indignant, flicking Ben with the wet towel.

'Ouch! That hurt! Just you wait . . .'

'Stop it, both of you,' Rosemary said angrily. 'You're behaving like children. Goodness, you've only been home a few days and already—'

Grateful for a diversion when the phone rang, Jane ran to answer it.

'It will be for me, anyway. I'm expecting a call from Rebecca. Oh, Mum, it's for you. Stephen. Why don't you invite him for dinner?' she mouthed, passing Rosemary the phone.

Hurtling upstairs in pursuit of his sister, Ben held his arms aloft like an aeroplane. He then began a noisy attempt at what was supposed to be a De Havilland comet. This was followed by a loud thump as something was thrown across the landing.

'What on earth's that noise?' Stephen's voice echoed down the line.

'Would you believe two university students supposedly revising for exams? In fact, just as you rang I was deliberating whether or not to take them back to nursery school. Ben, Jane, revision! And quietly.' Rosemary glowered at the two leering faces pressed between the banisters.

'Sounds chaotic. So how about escaping for supper tonight?'

'I'd love to, Stephen. It's a bit awkward at the moment. I don't suppose you'd like to come here instead?'

'That sounds nice.'

'Hmm. I don't know about nice. But it could be quite an experience. Shall we say 7.30, that's if you're prepared to risk it?'

Listening to the familiar click as Stephen hung up the phone, Rosemary's ears were assailed by two opposing styles of music. Bouncing off the bedroom walls it even appeared to reverberate down the stairs. Shaking her head in utter bewilderment as to how they could possibly revise listening to such a din, Rosemary retreated to the sanctuary of the kitchen and Radio 4.

'Mabel's here,' Ben called, peering from the hall window.

'Who's Mabel?'

'Stephen's car, dimbo!' Ben replied, looking in his sister's direction. 'Don't you know anything?'

Fortunately, Rosemary's warning glance in their direction meant dinner passed without incident.

With the meal drawing to a close Ben and Jane discussed their plans for the rest of the Easter vacation.

Rosemary looked disappointed. 'I thought you were both coming with me to the cottage.'

'Is that the place in Norfolk?' Stephen queried.

'Yes,' Ben groaned. 'And it's *boring*. Nothing but sea, sand and sky.'

'No, it's not,' Rosemary replied, indignant. 'You always loved it there when you were small. All those Easter egg hunts and—'

'Yes. But you forget we're not children any more, Mum,' Jane broke in kindly.

With raised eyebrows, Rosemary recalled the morning's bickering and subsequent wet towel fight on the landing.

'Really? Well, you could have fooled me.'

'Easter egg hunts?' Stephen asked, anxious to quell the developing tension.

In her usual garbled fashion, Jane explained how as children they used to go to the cottage every Easter. 'And Mum would hide Easter eggs and presents in the garden and we'd—'

'Mind you,' Ben interrupted, 'as we got older she made it jolly difficult for us. She used to leave a trail of cryptic clues, which we had to solve before we even got to our eggs.'

'What fun. I obviously had a deprived childhood,' Stephen chuckled. 'Unlike you two, I've never been on an Easter egg hunt in my life.'

With a mischievous gleam in his eye, Ben said matter-of-factly, 'Right, there you are, then, Mum. Problem solved. Take Stephen.'

Quick as a flash and agreeing with her brother for the very first time that day, Jane beamed. 'Why, of course. What a brilliant idea.'

The sound of a car's horn outside brought conversation to an abrupt halt.

'Come on, baby brother. Becky's here, if you want a lift?' Hurriedly gathering up some dishes, Jane took them through to the kitchen. To Rosemary's surprise, Ben followed suit.

'Bye, Mum. Bye, Stephen. See you later,' they called in unison.

'Phew!' Stephen gasped, in disbelief. 'Are they always like that?'

'No, not always. Sometimes they're even worse.' Draining the remains of her wine, Rosemary shook her head. 'To be fair, that's not quite true. I think it's more the pressure of work at the moment, only they won't admit to it. Ben's first-year exams and Jane's finals. I don't envy them at all. On the other hand, they have both been quite frightful today.'

'Perhaps you could do with another drink?'

'Definitely another drink and quite possibly a holiday.'

Refilling their two glasses, Stephen joined Rosemary on the sofa. Without thinking, she leaned her head against his shoulder.

'About Norfolk . . .' he said, fingering the raised cut crystal on his glass. 'I've never been to East Anglia before. With filming nearing completion, I reckon I could also do with a break. That's if you still intend to go . . . and want some company?'

Rosemary hesitated for a moment. 'Hmm. It's a bit like Ben said. There isn't a great deal to do at the cottage but it's certainly very relaxing. If you really want to come you'll be very welcome.'

'I'm positive. From where I'm sitting it sounds almost like heaven.' Placing his glass on the coffee table, Stephen reached for her hand. 'You know, Rosemary, I've been thinking for quite some time how nice it would be for us to share more than just a few snatched moments together. And . . .'

'And?' she ventured, worried what was coming next.

'I promise I shan't expect an Easter egg,' he teased, drawing her gently into his arms.

'Not even one containing cream eggs or chocolate buttons?'

'Chocolate buttons or cream eggs, eh? That sounds tempting. Almost as tempting as finding myself alone with you for once.' Stephen glanced towards the door. 'Even now I'm half-expecting Ben or Jane to come bounding through that doorway.'

'Oh, I think we shall be left in peace for a little while longer. Jane needs to discuss one of her English projects with Becky and Ben was going to a school reunion.'

'If that's anything like my school reunions, that probably means the pub and a game of darts.'

'Quite possibly,' Rosemary replied, slipping off her shoes. 'So why don't you sit back, relax, enjoy your wine and we can listen to the CD Jane bought me for my birthday. It's a replacement for a tape I once had. I played the original so much it became worn out. A bit like me at the moment.'

'Then you definitely need that holiday in Norfolk.'

Listening to the haunting strains of the young Canadian girl singing 'Save Me', Stephen stretched out his long legs. 'Mmm. Sit back and relax. You make that sound very tempting, Miss Felden. Perhaps I will . . . but only if you'll join me.'

'I suppose I might be tempted,' she murmured with a shy smile, easing herself by his side.

'Good. So how about this for starters?' he began, his lips brushing gently against hers.

Why was the English weather so unpredictable? Rosemary asked herself, gathering together last-minute bits and pieces. Since Easter it had been bitterly cold and now it even looked like rain.

'I hope you remembered to bring plenty of warm clothes,' she called to Stephen. 'There's no central heating and it can be jolly cold if the wind's coming straight in from the sea.'

Stephen looked up from where he was loading boxes into Rosemary's car. Mabel, they'd decided, was going to have a rest. 'I take it Ben and Jane got back to uni all right? Good heavens. What have you got in those boxes?'

'Just a few supplies,' came the nonchalant reply. 'You forget I'm taking you to the wilds of East Anglia.'

'In that case I dread to think what I'm letting myself in for. Now let me see. What have I been told so far? Sea, sand and nothing but sky; cold winds, no shops and no central heating. What a truly terrifying prospect.' Stephen pretended to reach into the boot for his travel bag. 'On reflection, I'm wondering if I ought to reconsider and change my mind?'

'Don't you dare! I couldn't possibly eat all that food by myself. Into the car with you, Stephen Walker.'

Delighted to obey, Stephen fixed her with a broad grin and fastened his seatbelt. 'Are you still happy about driving all the way?'

'Definitely. It's a route I know like the back of my hand. All you have to do is sit back and admire the view. By that I mean the road ahead,' she said, blushing, in reply to his earlier comment about how lovely she looked.

'Spoilsport,' came the murmured response.

For Stephen the East Anglian countryside was a whole new experience, totally unlike his native Sheffield. Villages and hamlets soon gave way to a vast expanse of flat fenland, dykes and fine black soil. The contrast between north Norfolk and the Peak District he knew so well was enormous.

Three hours later and by the light of the moon, they approached the nearest village to Romany Fields.

'That's Freda and Harry's cottage over there,' she said.

Turning to look over his shoulder, Stephen discerned a thin trail of smoke curling lethargically from a chimney pot to a star-laden sky. Intrigued, he wound down the car window to breathe in the pungent smell of wood smoke.

'With luck we can also have a nice log fire,' Rosemary began. 'Harry rang earlier to tell me he'd split some logs and Freda has made sure the beds are well aired and made up.'

With Stephen considering 'beds', as in plural, Rosemary slowed down to edge the car along a narrow track. 'Here goes,' she said with the faintest of smiles. 'This is where you say goodbye to civilization.'

Just as Rosemary had described on their first dinner date, Romany Fields appeared to be miles from anywhere.

'Of course you won't be able to appreciate the cottage in the dark,' she continued. 'Basically, it's typical Norfolk flint. Two up, two down, with a few recent additions.'

'What sort of additions?'

'A modern hot-water system, shower and a flush toilet. Before that it was a pump in the back garden and a chemical loo. Mum and Dad never seemed to mind the privations but I confess I like my creature comforts.'

'Do your parents still come here?' Stephen enquired. It was one thing knowing Ben and Jane were elsewhere but what about Rosemary's parents?

She put his mind at rest immediately. 'No. They don't come to stay any more. They can't manage the stairs with their arthritis. They're far happier with their new bungalow and the occasional SAGA holiday. Which was why they decided to give me the cottage in the first place. In case you're wondering, I didn't win the lottery. The mod cons are courtesy of royalties and film rights for *To Love the Hero*.'

Looking again in the direction of the cottage, Stephen saw a lamp shining in the window.

'Harry leaves it on for me so I can find the keyhole,' she said, switching off both the ignition and the car's headlights. 'Without it there could be quite a problem finding the front door, let alone the keyhole.'

Unlocking the door and flooding the porch with light, Rosemary returned to help Stephen with their bags and boxes. For a moment she stood perfectly still, listening to the rhythmic sound of the sea and waves gently dashing against the shore. In turn she breathed in the bracing salt-laced air.

'Oh, I do so love it here.'

Seeing her shiver, Stephen picked up the last of the boxes. 'Something tells me it's going to be a cold night. If that's the last of your few supplies, perhaps we'd better get inside.'

Before closing the door, Rosemary inhaled the air once more. 'With luck a cold night should mean fine weather tomorrow and the chance of a nice long walk. In the meantime, however, do you think you could light the fire?'

Unpacking the food, Rosemary prepared a quick and simple supper which they ate on their laps in front of a blazing log fire. Stephen, she noticed, seemed strangely pensive. 'Don't worry,' she said, breaking into his thoughts. 'I'll cook you a proper meal tomorrow.'

'A proper meal? This is a proper meal if you consider some of the things I've eaten lately. Quite often I'm simply too tired to cook after a long day's filming. Which is why I could possibly do with that walk you mentioned. Get rid of some of this excess weight.'

Rosemary raised her eyes in disbelief. From what little she'd seen of Stephen's tightly muscled frame during filming, there was little evidence of excess weight. Helping her clear away the dishes, he cast an admiring glance about the cottage interior.

'It all seems so idyllic. I really can't understand why Ben and Jane didn't want to come. It's so peaceful – almost like being in another world.'

'Exactly,' she said. 'And it's a world they no longer want to inhabit. The young aren't exactly renowned for wanting peace and quiet, are they?'

'Hold on a moment. I'm not exactly geriatric, you know.'

'I do know,' came the softly whispered reply. 'Don't forget I am seven years older than you, Stephen.'

Stephen bit his lip. Strangely enough they'd never really spoken of their age difference. Of course he was well aware of the disparity, only it had never occurred to him to discuss it. He moved to where she was putting cutlery away in a drawer.

'As far as I'm concerned there is no age difference. It's not something that bothers me Rosemary. Does it bother you?'

She thought for a moment before replying, 'I'm not sure. When I'm with you I never give it a thought. But . . .'

'But?'

'I often wonder what other people think, seeing us together.'

Stephen scowled and gave a derisive snort. 'I've long since given up caring what people think. It makes life a hell of a lot easier. Surely we're all that matter? Aren't we?'

'I'd like to think so,' she said, looking up into his deeply earnest face.

Kissing the top of her head, Stephen pulled her close, feeling the warmth of her body through his shirt. Yes. It was exactly as he'd described a few moments ago. Like being in another world. Another world where only he and Rosemary existed. A whole weekend with her to himself and *definitely* no interruptions from Jane or Ben.

At length Rosemary gave a tiny yawn and, moving reluctantly from his embrace, placed the fireguard in front of the fire and took some candles and matches from a drawer. 'In case of power cuts,' she explained. 'They always happen here when you're least expecting it.'

Stephen's expression altered quite dramatically. Spying the candles and matches in her hand, he said 'If you don't mind I'd prefer a torch. I noticed one in the boot when I was loading the car.'

Initially bewildered, Rosemary froze with horror. Of course

– the candles. How could she be so stupid? She remembered the burned-out shell of the house in Sheffield and Stephen's friend, who'd died in the fire.

'Oh, Stephen. How insensitive of me. Yes, you're right. There is a torch in the boot and also some spare batteries.'

Suffused with embarrassmet, she handed him both the keys to her car and the cottage. Leaving Stephen to lock up, she went to her bedroom.

On arrival they'd put Stephen's bag in the room once used by the children. At the time Rosemary had been too timid to discuss sleeping arrangements.

'How do you tell someone you want to go to bed with them?' she asked her reflection in the mirror. 'Especially when you've only ever slept with one man and that was your husband?'

Trying to ignore their difference in ages, plus the fact that Stephen could have his pick of dozens of women, Rosemary's mind was in turmoil. Deep down she felt sure Stephen was fond of her. Exactly how fond, she was yet to find out. Slipping out of her clothes, she shivered and retrieved a long winceyette nightdress (a must for cold, solitary nights at Romany Fields) and put it on.

Hearing footsteps on the gravel below, she switched off the bedroom light and went to the window. In the pale glow of moonlight she saw Stephen take the torch from the boot, check the batteries and lock the car. Then, turning his gaze upwards in the direction of her bedroom window, he returned to the cottage.

Rosemary meanwhile paused in the shadows before making her way towards the bed. Stephen, she discerned, had already locked the cottage door and was at this very moment climbing the stairs. For a brief moment his footsteps appeared to halt outside her room, but were followed by the distinctive click of the children's bedroom door and then everything was silent.

With earlier thoughts of sleep denied her, Rosemary tossed and turned restlessly. Eventually, reminded that she'd not opened the bedroom window for fear of drawing attention to herself when Stephen was at the car, she tiptoed from the bed.

Drawing back the curtains and opening the window, shafts of pale silvery moonlight filled the room with deep shadows. Grateful for the sudden rush of cool night air that caused her to shiver, Rosemary acknowledged that at least it had the desired effect. That of clearing the confusion in her head and the uncontrollable pounding in her breast.

At length, having regulated her breathing to correspond with the rhythmic beating of the waves upon the shore, she leaned her elbows against the window-sill and closed her eyes. 'Oh, Stephen,' she whispered, her voice barely audible as the shifting seas drowned out not only her plaintive sigh but also that of her bedroom door opening. Only when she felt the curtains brush against her face was she aware of his presence.

Turning, Rosemary saw him silhouetted in the doorway, the renewed drumming in her heart now completely out of control. Anxious that he shouldn't see the abject panic on her face, she turned back to face the window.

'I – er – couldn't sleep,' she faltered. 'I thought some air might help.'

'Me too,' he acknowledged huskily, moving noiselessly behind her until she felt his warm breath on the nape of her neck. 'Rosemary . . . I want you so much—'

Relief flooded Stephen's face when she turned and held out her hand. In no time at all he bent to kiss her, swept her lovingly into his arms and carried her to the bed.

'Rosemary. My dear, sweet love,' he moaned, cupping her face gently in his hands.

For a while he held her protectively in his embrace and only when her breathing became more steadied did he hold her at arm's length. Slowly . . . very slowly . . . he began to unbutton her nightdress.

With a soft, muffled swish of fabric, the nightdress fell to the floor, closely followed by Stephen's T-shirt and boxer shorts. Rosemary's breath caught in her throat as he drew her towards him once more.

'Stephen . . I . . . it's been such a long time since —'

'Shh,' he whispered reassuringly, placing a finger across her lips. 'I understand.'

Silencing her untold fears with a series of kisses, Stephen's lips and gentle hands moved expertly over her body, releasing a deep longing she'd quite forgotten existed. Fleetingly reminded of Gary's less than considerate lovemaking, she pushed all thoughts of her unfaithful husband to the back of her mind and gave herself up completely. After years filled with pain and anguish, she was like a prisoner suddenly set free of her chains.

In the early morning, when Stephen reached for her again, their bodies came together as one. Sated and content, they slept once more, wrapped in each other's arms.

Much later, it was the warm glow of dappled sunlight dancing on her face that caused Rosemary to open her eyes and look about her. Stephen was sleeping peacefully by her side, his hair ruffled and unkempt, falling across his face.

With a tentative gesture she put out her hand, wanting to stroke it away from his cheek. Fearful that she might wake him and suddenly conscious of her nakedness, she slid modestly beneath the covers, all manner of thoughts racing through her head. Perhaps she should try and creep downstairs and have a shower before he woke? Making love by moonlight was one thing. Waking up the next morning in brilliant sunshine was another. It was also strangely disconcerting.

Stephen stirred, aware of her trying to coax her own short hair into place with her fingers.

'Leave it,' he said sleepily. 'You look quite lovely. Not at all like the demure Jane Eyre I took to bed last night.'

'Why Jane Eyre?'

'You in that enormous nightdress of yours. I thought I was never going to find you.'

I'm glad you did, Rosemary thought, her body glowing at the memory of him deftly unfastening seemingly endless buttons in voluminous folds of fabric.

Knowing the same nightdress was now lying in a crumpled heap on the bedroom floor, and feeling a sudden chill breeze blowing in from the open window, she pulled the duvet up to her shoulders and announced, 'For your information, nightdresses like that are a must at Romany Fields, particularly in winter. There's no central heating here, don't forget. I suppose you're going to tell me you northerners never feel the cold.'

'Aye, lass. 'Appen we don't,' he joked, sitting up in bed, exposing his naked torso. 'When thou's used to washing in t'back yard after coming home from t'mill.'

Realizing he was making fun of his childhood, Rosemary giggled. 'You surely don't expect me to believe it was that bad? Don't forget I saw all those family photos at your sister's.'

'So you did ... although we never had central heating either.' Fixing her with one of his melting smiles, Stephen pushed his hair from his face. Their childhoods must have been so different. Yet whose was the happiest?

'Central heating or not, I'm going to have a shower and get us some breakfast,' Rosemary said before moving away, then added as an afterthought, 'And as you were so rude about my Jane Eyre nightdress, I shall borrow your T-shirt instead.'

Throwing back the duvet, Stephen reached out and passed it to her. 'If you must know I'm deeply indebted to Jane Eyre. One of my first major roles in rep was as Edward Rochester.'

'With your eyes and hair? You're not dark enough to be Mr Rochester.'

'There's such things as contact lenses, you know. Besides, you should have seen me in my wig and side whiskers. Quite a sight I was.'

'And quite a sight you are now,' she quipped, her eyes scanning his naked body. 'So, what's it to be, Mr Rochester, and how do you want it?'

In reply to his raised eyebrows and wicked smile, she said hurriedly 'I meant tea or coffee? Black or white?'

'Guess.'

Rosemary's eyes sparkled playfully, as she called out to him, ''appen it'll be tea then,' and ducked as he threw a pillow in her direction.

Chapter 10

Leaving Stephen with his tea, Rosemary headed for the shower. He, meanwhile, took stock of his surroundings. Last night in the moonlight this room had been merely a blur of distorted shapes and shadows. The bedroom itself wasn't large. Apart from a brass bedstead, bentwood chair and some shelves, there was only a simple wash-stand, complete with china jug and basin. With no space for a wardrobe, a small alcove had been screened off in the same floral print as the curtains – he presumed for Rosemary's clothes.

Far removed from her small yet elegant family house in the home counties, Stephen studied Rosemary's selection of books, photos and sentimental treasures displayed upon the shelves. There was no need to ask her about her life. It was all here in this room.

A shuttered look came over Stephen's face. How different from his own flat, where his walls, unlike Rosemary's, were practically bare. They divulged nothing of his life, past or present. Quite simply because there was little he wished to be reminded of. Nothing he cared for other than a single family photograph album, kept in a bedside cabinet.

After breakfast, when Rosemary suggested a walk, Stephen

agreed immediately. Weeks of filming had left him mentally and physically drained. Now, with the sun shining brightly in a vast expanse of azure-blue sky, he breathed in great gulps of ozone-laced air and reached for Rosemary's hand. What was it she'd also said? With the Easter holidays over and this part of the coastline well away from the main tourist trap . . . What could be more perfect than being alone with her?

Newly invigorated, Stephen bent down to kiss the top of her head, a warm glow pervading his body. Saying nothing, Rosemary simply looked up at him and smiled. There was no need for words. It was almost as if her own relaxed state of being (a far cry from the tense, nervous woman he'd taken to bed last night) had transmitted itself through their entwined fingertips.

Strolling hand in hand, Rosemary took great delight in pointing out assorted wildlife, numerous wild flowers and nesting sites of visiting birds. Stephen was fascinated. His attention drawn to a bird singing high on the wing, he learned how the drier slacks of dunes provided the ideal nesting spot for skylarks.

Moments later, approaching large clumps of yellow ragwort, Rosemary explained, 'It won't be long now before these are all covered in cinnabar caterpillars.'

Stephen grimaced, reminded of the dreaded cabbage-white caterpillars that plagued his father's vegetables.

'Oh, but you'd love these,' she said playfully. 'They might begin life as Watford supporters but they soon transfer their allegiance to The Blades.'

Stephen turned to follow her footsteps into the sand dunes. 'You've lost me, I'm afraid. I haven't a clue what you're talking about.'

'The cinnabar. From black and yellow caterpillars they

transform into magnificent black and scarlet moths. Although some purists might argue black and vermilion. In case you were wondering . . . not all moths come out at night.'

'Moths, butterflies. I wouldn't know the difference anyway,' Stephen remarked with a grin. 'But do carry on. I'm really enjoying today's nature lesson.'

At lunchtime, and with the strain of recent weeks lifting from their shoulders, Rosemary drove into the nearest hamlet. Without explanation she left Stephen in the car, only to return clutching two warm packages, the mouth-watering aroma of fish and chips wafting through folds of creamy-white paper.

'Lunch,' she said, heading back in the direction of the cottage. 'You'll have to let me know if it's as good as Harry Ramsden's.'

Back at Romany Fields, where it was still sunny enough to sit in the garden to eat, they tucked in eagerly. Neither having realized just how hungry they were, it also wasn't long before Stephen fell asleep.

Hardly surprising, Rosemary thought to herself. Most first-time visitors to the region found the air here unusually strong. Also strong were the hands that had so lovingly taken her in his arms before they'd made love. Hands which Rosemary now covered with a tartan rug, leaving the remainder to fall gently over Stephen's knees.

Filled with a renewed yearning and the now-familiar tingling in the pit of her stomach, she tiptoed away. This simply won't do, she told herself. Don't forget, there's work to be done.

For a while, working on the revised first draft of her new novel, Rosemary was lost in another world, that of the 1920s. It was only when she paused to flex her wrists, stretch her legs and make a cup of coffee that her thoughts turned to Laura Carr. Brushing away a tiny cobweb from the corner of Laura's New York postcard, pinned to the corkboard in the kitchen, Rosemary was reminded of their recent conversation.

Laura had phoned from America before Easter. Anxious for news of Rosemary and the children, she also enquired after the latest Romy Felden manuscript. As usual Rosemary had expressed her doubts concerning the current typescript. There was no guarantee it was what the publishers wanted. Laura in turn had berated her friend most severely. Having had what she termed a *satisfactory* working relationship with Gary Fielding, Laura had in fact loathed Rosemary's husband. Many's the time she'd been secretly appalled at the way he treated his wife.

Never one to speak ill of the dead, Laura had always chosen to keep her thoughts to herself. This time, however, she forgot herself.

'Stop putting yourself down, Rosemary. That control freak of a husband is no longer around. Of course it's what Farmer and Butler want. Your first three books are simply flying off the shelves here. American readers can't get enough of you. I do wish you'd come over and see it for yourself.'

Already prepared for Rosemary's excuses, Laura had drawn some comfort from the progress report on the new novel and filming of *To Love the Hero*. She'd also registered the amount of times Stephen Walker's name had come into the conversation. Hmm, she'd thought, deeply intrigued, telling herself not to pry. Rosemary was such a dark horse (look how she'd kept secret the fact that she was Romy Felden). On the other hand, wasn't Oliver planning to return to the States during Easter? Determining to invite Oliver and his wife for supper the moment he arrived, Laura had said her farewells.

'OK, for now I will accept your excuses. I'll also ask you to accept mine for sounding off at you like that. In American parlance I've just experienced *the most godawful day*. In the meantime, as they also say over here, I guess I'll have to take a rain check on you visiting the Big Apple. Just make sure you come soon.'

Perhaps I will now, Rosemary resolved, washing and drying her coffee cup and saucer. Being with Stephen had somehow filled her with a new-found confidence and self-esteem.

Smiling to herself at how different her life was without Gary – very twenty-first century as opposed to being married to a Victorian-style bully – Rosemary made a grab for the phone, anxious not to wake her sleeping guest.

Reassured to find it was only Harry ringing to see if she needed more logs, Rosemary told him there were plenty and that everything else at the cottage was in order. Except for taking the all-important backup and switching off her laptop, she reminded herself, before turning her attention to dinner. In no time at all the table was laid, the Chardonnay was in the fridge (with the smoked salmon) and the Merlot breathing nicely in readiness for the steak.

For a brief moment when he awoke, Stephen was completely disoriented by the unfamiliar scenery. It took the distant murmuring of the sea and the warbling of a solitary skylark overhead to remind him of his location. Where was Rosemary? Surprised to find himself covered by a rug, he disentangled himself, conscious of the lengthening shadows of afternoon and the distant chink of china from the kitchen. How long had he been asleep? What on earth must Rosemary be thinking?

'Rosemary, I do apologize. How rude of me to fall asleep

and leave you with all this.'

'Nonsense,' she replied, looking up from where she was folding dinner napkins and arranging the tray for afternoon tea. 'You looked as if you were in dire need of a rest and I should have warned you the air here is pretty strong. I thought it would do you good to forget all about Oliver for a few hours.'

'A few hours! How long have I been asleep?'

Motioning to a clock on the wall, Rosemary took the tray into the cosy sitting room, where she'd lit the fire. With another look at the clock, Stephen rubbed his eyes. Was that really the time? No wonder he was feeling better.

'I've been admiring your collection of books, CDs and tapes,' he said, sitting down on a bulging settee. 'Am I correct in assuming there's no television?'

'Right first time. Much to Ben and Jane's disapproval, television is banned at Romany Fields. Although I do know they used to pop across to Harry and Freda's for a crafty look. As for myself, I find music and books far more relaxing.'

'If I feel any more relaxed I shan't want to go back to the studios.'

Watching him stretch contentedly, Rosemary played with the lacy corner of the tray cloth. 'You're welcome to come and stay again . . . that's if you'd like to?'

'I'd like that very much,' he said, his voice husky, turning steady grey eyes in her direction.

After dinner they returned once more to the open fire, Stephen sitting in an armchair, Rosemary on a large cushion at his feet. In silence they watched myriad amber and gold flames lick and curl their way up the chimney, while outside in the moonlight spray-kissed waves lapped gently against the shore.

'Do you spend much time here by yourself?'

Her answer was not unexpected. 'As often as I can now that Ben and Jane are at uni. To me being at Romany Fields is like escaping to another world.'

'Don't you ever get lonely?'

'Definitely not. It's the peace and solitude I come for. Unlike yourself, I was an only child. Besides,' she continued wistfully, looking towards the bookshelves, 'who can feel lonely sharing a house with the Brontës, Austen and Keats?'

'You never felt deprived of company as a child?'

'Not that I was aware of. According to my father, when I wasn't tearing about the dunes like a gypsy, I always had my head buried in a book. Don't they say playing on your own encourages the imagination? Perhaps that's why I can write. Correction. Change that to why I *think* I can write.'

'I don't think, I know,' Stephen told her. 'I thought *To Love the Hero* extremely well written and you remember what Mary said about it that day in Sheffield.'

Rosemary leaned back against his knees. 'Thank God Oliver liked it too. Otherwise we wouldn't be sitting here now. Still, enough about my childhood. What about yours? It must have been very different for you, surrounded and cosseted by your sisters.'

'Yes, I suppose it was. Like you say, you're never aware of these things at the time.'

'And what do you suppose they think of you spending the weekend with an older woman?'

'For a start, it's none of their business. Secondly, you're as old as you feel.'

'That's all right then,' Rosemary replied, ignoring the slightly abrasive edge to his voice. 'Because at this very moment I feel like a foolish sixteen-year-old.'

'Really? Then let me see . . . by my calculations that must make me old enough to be your father.'

Unaware she was treading on dangerous ground, Rosemary continued without thinking. 'Are your family used to you having affairs with older women?'

Almost immediately Stephen pulled away. 'No, Rosemary. They aren't. Despite what you might have heard . . . or read, I am *not* in the habit of having affairs with women of any age.'

Realizing only too late she'd hurt his feelings (she knew she shouldn't have had that last glass of wine), Rosemary was filled with remorse. 'Stephen, forgive me. I didn't mean to sound so offensive. I merely thought . . . You know . . .'

'Only too well,' Stephen said with a derisive snort. 'As I've said before, never believe all you read in the papers.'

For a few embarrassing moments the room was plunged into silence, save for the crackle of logs in the grate. With an anguished groan, Stephen reached down to clasp her hand. 'My turn to apologize, I think.'

'There's really no need.'

'Ah, but there is. I had no right to snap at you like that. However, if it's confessions you're after . .'

'Confessions? No, I didn't mean that at all.'

Stephen, it appeared, seemed suddenly determined to see this conversation through. First, however, he reached down and pulled her gently to her feet so that she could sit on his lap. Next he caressed her cheek and tenderly kissed her forehead.

'Right. So . . . shall we begin with the early days when I was working in the foundry in Sheffield? I'll admit there were a few girls then, but I was no different from other lads my age – and of course that was before I got married.'

'You're married?' Rosemary gasped. She'd never given it a

thought. How could she be so naïve? Stephen Walker had a wife!

'No. Don't pull away from me,' he said, taking her firmly by the shoulders. 'It isn't what you're thinking. I was married once and now I'm not. That's the truth.'

'And children . . . do you have any children?'

'No,' he replied bitterly. 'Would you believe I fell for the oldest trick in the book? She told me she was pregnant and I insisted on doing the decent thing by marrying her. After the wedding took place it was only a matter of weeks before I found out it was all a lie. She only wanted the wedding ring on her finger so she could give up work and go out gallivanting with her other married friends.'

'Stephen. How cruel. Whatever did you do?'

'At the time nothing, I was only nineteen. I don't mind admitting it wasn't exactly easy playing the part of dutiful husband, but I did my best. Then, one night when I'd been working the night shift and came home early – I'd gashed my finger you see . . .'

When Stephen began rubbing unconsciously at a pale white scar on his forefinger, Rosemary half-suspected where all this was leading. 'What happened?' she questioned hesitantly.

'I found her in bed with one of my old school-friends.'

'Some school-friend.'

Stephen glared and glanced away. 'Aye. You could say that. Although in the end I suppose he turned out to be a very good friend indeed. Thanks to him I was at least able to divorce her for adultery. As for him, poor devil, he also felt duty bound to marry her.'

Marginally reassured by this news, Rosemary still needed to know the all-important question. 'And, er, do you still see her?'

'No. Thank God. They emigrated to Australia and we lost contact. At least I hoped we had. Wanting to get away from it all, I eventually decided to join the rep. It was a good way of channelling all that pent-up emotion. Though I say it myself, and thanks to playwrights like John Osborne, I became quite adept at playing angry young men. Unfortunately, once I'd started to make a name for myself as an actor things began to turn nasty.'

In response to Rosemary's questioning frown, Stephen hissed angrily. 'Maggie, my ex-wife, thought she could make some money by contacting the press. They in turn sent some slimy reporter sniffing round the theatre. At first they tried to make out I was as unpleasant as some of the characters I was playing. When that failed Maggie came up trumps with some truly Oscar-winning performance of her own. Not only did she tell the reporter I'd made her have an abortion—'

'Even though she'd never been pregnant?'

'That's not the end of it,' Stephen continued, his eyes hard as flints. 'She also said I was a wife-beater and a drunk. And if that pack of lies wasn't enough, that bastard of a reporter set me up with . . . You can guess what I'm going to say, can't you? Let's face it, there's always some cheap little bimbo prepared to put herself in a compromising situation, just to sell a story and make a name for herself.'

From the look on Rosemary's face, Stephen could see that she was horrified. Slowly he released his hold on her and raked his fingers roughly through his hair.

'But if it wasn't true and you were set-up, surely you could have—'

'Defended myself or sued. Yes I suppose I could but things were different back then. Now I don't give a damn and the press know it. For the most part they leave me alone these days. As for that disastrous set-up with my ex-agent, I really should have known better and trusted my gut instincts on that occasion.'

Disastrous set-up, Rosemary thought to herself. Was that the result of the article she'd seen ages ago, when she'd been staying with Sarah? Stephen confirmed her suspicions.

'My agent suggested I take this young starlet to a film première. I told him I didn't want to do it – my father had been taken ill – but he insisted. It was good publicity, he told me. Add a bit of glamour to the occasion.'

'And did it?'

'Hardly. You know the sort. A typical wannabe. She ate too much, talked too much and drank too much, which was in stark contrast to the dress she was wearing. There wasn't too much of that! Then, to add insult to injury, at the end of the evening she announced to the waiting press that we were engaged.'

'I take it you weren't?'

'Definitely not! The only engagement that took place was an appointment with my agent, telling him of my decision to disinstruct him. With my contract up for renewal anyway, it all worked out quite nicely.'

Quite nicely wasn't exactly how Rosemary would have defined this distressing saga. Instead, it only served to remind her how gullible she'd been to believe all the earlier stories relating to Stephen's behaviour. Her eyes filled with remorse and sadness.

'I think that's wicked, absolutely wicked. To think your ex-wife could do that to you. As for your agent . . Your career could have been ruined.'

'Ex-agent,' Stephen corrected, brushing a solitary tear away from her cheek with the pad of his thumb. 'Aye, you're right,

Maggie very nearly succeeded. Still you know what they say about Yorkshire grit and determination? I only hope all the sacrifices I made for my career have been worth it.'

'What sort of sacrifices?'

'A loyal wife, children and a proper home.'

Rosemary forced a weak smile. 'At least you've proved yourself to be a one-woman man?'

Stephen raised an eyebrow. It was only when he heard the word 'Mabel' his face lit up. 'Yes, of course. Good old Mabel. Ever faithful, ever true,' he conceded.

Once more cradled in his arms, Rosemary said, 'I had no idea ... I'm truly sorry for opening up old wounds. From experience I know only too well how painful they can be. Do you think perhaps we could try and heal them together?'

Stephen squeezed her hand. 'I'd like to think we can. So, there you have it. If nothing else perhaps you'll forgive me for being so pig-headed when we first met. I confess when I kept hearing Oliver talk about you and the success of your books, I felt almost resentful. It was as if everything had been so easy for you.'

'How do you feel about me now?'

'Isn't that obvious?' came the murmured reply as his lips met hers.

Releasing her from his embrace, Stephen straightened the shawl she had draped about her shoulders. It was the one she'd worn the day they went to the Apostles' Pond. He saw it all now. That's why she'd reacted so strangely to the word betrayal. Yes. They had both been betrayed. Was that what brought them together now?

Watching his fingers smooth the soft folds of fabric, Rosemary's own thoughts went winging back to that eventful day.

'You never did say who I reminded you of when I wore this shawl.'

'At the time I was going to say Georgiana, the heroine in your novel. Since spending this weekend with you and getting to know you better, I'd say you're a mixture of Georgiana, Cathy from *Wuthering Heights* and Jane Eyre all rolled into one.'

Rosemary made no answer. Mesmerized by a cascade of tiny red sparks settling in the sooty black expanse of chimney, she was transported back to her childhood. What was it her father used to say when that happened? *'The fairies are coming, Rosemary. They're coming to grant you three wishes.'* What would she wish for tonight?

Calling to mind all the solitary nights she'd spent at the cottage listening to the wind moaning down the chimney, Rosemary thought how strange that Stephen should have mentioned two of her favourite books, *Wuthering Heights* and *Jane Eyre*. Only last autumn, trying to come to terms with both her babies being at university, she'd sat in this very room imagining herself first as the wild and wilful Cathy, searching for Heathcliff, and then the tragic Jane, bereft at leaving Rochester and Thornfield Hall.

Though the stories were different, (particularly since the painful discovery of Gary's infidelity), Rosemary frequently likened their combined sadness and despair to that of her own existence. Even now she wasn't ashamed to admit that along with her writing it was escaping to other worlds, particularly those inhabited by Jane and Cathy, that had helped maintain her sanity. Wondering if Stephen would think her foolish if she divulged her innermost thoughts, she realized there was no need. When she turned to look deep into his eyes, she saw he understood perfectly.

Moving to one side and easing himself from the armchair, Stephen walked to the bookshelf and picked up a volume of Jane Austen. 'Would you like me to read to you?'

'Yes. But not that if you don't mind. I'd much prefer the Keats.'

When the anthology fell open at *The Eve of St Agnes*, Rosemary nestled back against him with a deep sigh of contentment. With the logs burning through and the glowing embers fading into grey, she listened to his resonant voice breathe life into every line, until at length, exactly like Porphyro and Madeline, they slipped quietly into the night and became lovers once more.

When Sunday afternoon and the time for their departure arrived all too quickly, Rosemary was filled with mixed emotions. It had been a truly wonderful weekend. Even this morning had been a huge success. Following yet another invigorating walk, they'd lunched at the local pub on freshly caught seafood. In turn, Stephen had been introduced to mine host and his special brew, Harry and some of the locals. One in particular had caught Stephen's eye.

Winking at Rosemary, he whispered, 'I knew a remarkable character actor in rep exactly like that. He played the perfect Barkus from Dickens' *David Copperfield*.'

Greatly amused by the old chap sitting in the inglenook, puffing away on a pipe, Stephen half-expected him to announce, 'Barkus is willing' to the rosy-cheeked barmaid of Peggoty-sized proportions. He'd then shown his own willingness by buying Harry and his friends a drink. For the first time in years he didn't even mind being the focus of attention. At least these voyeurs were only raising their glasses of beer in his direction, not telephoto lenses.

Rosemary suppressed a smile; doubtless tongues would be wagging the following week. Mrs Fielding had never been seen with a man before, other than her husband or father.

'She certainly do look happy. An' that young man o' hers was very nice an' bought us all a drink,' Harry was to announce to Freda on his return for her traditional Sunday roast. 'Not like that stuck up husband o' hers who used to look down his nose at us an' talk nothin' but squit.'

Locking the door of the cottage, Rosemary watched Stephen place what remained of the boxes in the boot.

'At least there's not as many as when we arrived,' he remarked. 'I can't believe how much I've eaten this weekend.'

'I thought you were quite adept at shifting boxes? Or are you forgetting those you took to your friend at Swallow Park.'

Stephen looked suddenly guilty. 'Ah, Swallow Park. I think perhaps it's confession time again. I don't know anyone at Swallow Park, Rosemary. The boxes were empty. It was simply an excuse to see you again.'

She stared at him, open-mouthed. 'But you said . . . You mean you loaded Mabel with empty boxes and drove all that way just to see me? What if I hadn't been at home?'

Stephen shrugged his shoulders. 'It was a risk I was prepared to take.'

'Was it worth it?' she asked, looking earnestly into his face.

'Oh, yes. Most definitely yes.'

Once on their way home, Rosemary watched Stephen insert her favourite disc into the CD player. How appropriate she thought, when the words, 'Just a kiss, I have lived for this, just a smile, hold me captive for a while,' echoed from the rear speakers.

When Stephen had kissed her and taken her so lovingly in his arms, she'd wanted that to last for more than a while. All too soon, however, she knew they must return to reality. Stephen to the studios and Rosemary to her writing.

Pulling up outside her house, she began to dread the moment when they would have to say goodbye. Even now her stomach was in knots.

'Don't forget Oliver's party,' Stephen called, transferring his bag to Mabel's boot. 'Can I suggest you wear that little black number you wore to our first date? I want everyone to see how stunning you look.'

Rosemary was deeply moved. Standing there dressed in denims and a navy and white striped fleece (a result of succumbing to Jane's insistence that she *wasn't* too old to wear jeans), the last thing on her mind was the black dress. Feeling a tug at her heart, she watched Stephen climb into his car and switch on the ignition. Mabel, to their surprise, started like a dream.

'You see, Mabel's enjoyed her weekend too.'

'Not half as much as me,' Stephen called from the open window, reaching for her hand and holding it to his lips. Then, all too soon and with a final wave, he was gone.

Grateful for the diversion (at least it helped stem the tears), Rosemary immersed herself in the post she found waiting on the doormat. Bills and junk mail apart there were two very welcome letters to lift her spirits. Blue airmail from Laura in America and cream vellum from Sarah in Wales, both imploring her to go and stay. Sarah to the renewed peace and calm of the Welsh hills, now that the panic of lambing was well behind them, and Laura to the delights of New York. At the bottom of Laura's letter was a scribbled postscript.

'P.S. Rosemary, dear, I've just had the weirdest invitation to a party from a Suzanne and Wally Milburn. They say they are friends of yours – you met in London? Anyway, they've sent me this invi-

tation and suggest I try and persuade you to come too. So – how about it? Can I twist your arm? Will you venture across the Pond to the Big A? Please ring me. L.'

Suzanne and Wally, Rosemary reflected. She hadn't thought of them in ages. Fancy contacting Laura when she hadn't even given them her address. She could only assume, therefore, that the kindly Americans she'd met at the V&A all those weeks ago had made some enquiries via Farmer and Butler in New York.

Chapter 11

In their hotel room on the outskirts of Heathrow, Rosemary and Stephen prepared for Oliver's party, the chosen venue for tonight's celebrations being the banqueting suite at Pinewood Studios. Oliver had taken his wife there several years ago when the company concerned had provided a champagne reception, followed by three-course dinner and entertainment. Miriam had been enthralled. Sharing a love of opera, the guests were entertained between courses by members of the Royal Opera House and Oliver had even put in a request for Miriam's favourite duet from *The Pearl Fishers*.

Already wearing the requested black dress, Rosemary was in the process of fastening her own pearls when Stephen produced a maroon velvet box containing an Art Deco brooch and matching earrings.

'They're based on a design by the architect Otto Wagner,' he said. 'I know you'd originally planned to wear pearls but I wanted you to have something special – from me. They might help inspire you to finish the new novel. Didn't you say you had writer's block?'

Rosemary smiled, delighted, admiring the bold geometric shapes of silver and black onyx.

'Stephen, they are *beautiful*. And absolutely perfect for getting me in the mood of the 20s and 30s.' She refrained from adding it wasn't writer's block preventing her from finishing her typescript, it was wanting to spend every waking moment with him instead.

'And you look beautiful, too,' he replied, helping her with the pin on the brooch. 'It might interest you to know I'm also in the mood, but not for the 20s and 30s. In a way I wish we weren't going out. Do you suppose they'd miss us?'

'They most certainly would,' Rosemary scolded, feeling Stephen's fingers brush seductively against her throat. 'I don't think Oliver would be very pleased to find his leading man absent from the proceedings.'

'Spoilsport,' Stephen said, turning his attention to his bow-tie.

Suppressing a deep yearning to go along with Stephen's suggestion and remain in the hotel, Rosemary clipped on the earrings and stepped forward to help adjust his tie. What a transformation.

Gone was his usual casual array of clothes and in their place a superbly tailored dinner suit. If only she'd been able to persuade Ben to wear something similar to a recent black-tie function at Sheffield. As expected there'd been a resounding, 'No way!'

Also as expected, an ecstatic Oliver greeted everyone affectionately. After weeks of arduous filming, illness, niggling problems and temperamental actors, he was delighted to have everything in the can. Gone were the clapperboards, cables, lights and props and people in nineteenth-century costumes, and in their place elegantly dressed guests waiting to enjoy a relaxed evening of excellent food, fine wine and above all good company.

Seeing Rosemary and Stephen arrive together only confirmed earlier rumours of previous weeks. So it was true. Romy Felden (who'd already won the affection of cast and crew) and the infamous Stephen Walker were an item. Astonished by Stephen's recent transformation, there were those who'd also asked themselves how on earth Rosemary had managed it. They'd been even more surprised to discover a hidden warmth and tenderness beneath that steel-hard exterior.

'Rosemary, honey, you are looking *gorgeous*,' Oliver said, finding her on her own. 'Just like Miriam always says, you can't beat the little black dress. I only wish she were here to tell you herself. Now, why aren't you drinking? Let me get you another glass of champagne.'

Knowing it was useless to protest (she didn't much care for champagne – like red wine, just one glass too many gave her a headache), Rosemary watched Oliver stop a passing waiter.

'You can tell me to mind my own business if you like,' he continued, thrusting a glass in her hand, 'but you and Stephen . . . you certainly make a swell couple. Tell me, is it serious?'

Rosemary cast a furtive eye in Stephen's direction. Though wanting to remain together, they had agreed to separate for a while, if only to do the necessary mingling. Stephen, she observed, was already in animated conversation with Fergus and Gemma.

'I'm not exactly sure what you mean by serious, Oliver. All I know is that I am very fond of him and that we also enjoy each other's company.'

Seemingly content with her response, Oliver made a mental note to speak to Stephen before the end of the evening. Perhaps something along the lines of a fatherly chat was in order.

'Say! A little bird tells me there's a new book in the pipeline, so shall we drink to that? What is it, by the way, another Regency?'

Taking a reluctant sip of champagne, Rosemary placed her glass on a nearby table, leaving her fingers free to caress the Art Deco brooch. 'No. This time I'm writing about the 1920s and 30s. After that I'm planning to go right back in time to Medieval England.'

Watching her host quaff half his champagne, Rosemary could only assume he didn't share her problem. Either that or tomorrow morning he'd be waking up with one hell of a headache.

Oliver smacked his lips appreciatively and reached for a canapé, all the while recalling Stephen in the role of a tourney knight at the court of Richard the Lionheart.

'Medieval England, eh? I see,' he said, fixing her with a huge grin. 'Is that just coincidence or just *a cunning plan*, as old Baldrick would say, to keep Stephen in work once he's finished filming in the States? Let me know when the book's finished. Maybe we could turn that into a mini-series, too.'

Oliver studied Rosemary's reaction over the rim of his glass. To his surprise she didn't appear to be listening. As far as she was concerned, everything in the room had gone black. It was as if she'd been stabbed in the heart. Stephen going to America? Surely not? All the time they'd spent together in recent weeks and he hadn't mentioned it once.

Spying her ashen face, Oliver downed the remains of his drink and began to panic. 'Gee, honey, I'm sorry. You mean you didn't know? Jeez! I guess I'd better go and have a word with Stephen.'

Watching his departing figure, Rosemary stared after him, unable to make any sense of what she'd just heard. Numbed, and against her better judgement, she reached for her own glass, took a deep gulp and gazed about her. Oliver had already broken into Fergus and Stephen's conversation, leaving the two men in earnest consultation. She meanwhile attempted small talk with Gemma and one of the wardrobe mistresses but it was no use. Her mind wasn't focussing, her attention was elsewhere. What was Oliver saying to Stephen?

'Stephen, sorry for butting in, but this is important. What exactly are you doing about Rosemary?'

'Doing about. . . ? I've done nothing to upset her, if that's what you're implying?'

'Hold on, I'm not accusing you of anything. Anyone can see the two of you get along real swell. In fact, I've never seen her look so darned happy. Only I don't want to see her hurt, Stephen. Rosemary's a very dear friend and she's been hurt too much already. I knew her husband, don't forget.'

Stephen shrugged his shoulders in complete bewilderment. What was the fellow rambling on about, or had Oliver had too much to drink? 'For what it's worth,' he replied, his tone defensive, 'you have my word. I would never hurt Rosemary.'

Sensing Stephen was about to walk away, Oliver put a restraining hand on his arm. 'Maybe not intentionally. I'll even go so far as saying that thanks to you she looks like a new woman – but you haven't told her about your contract in the States, have you?'

'My contract? No. I was planning to tell her tonight, once we were alone.'

Looking across the crowded room, Stephen registered the hurt and disbelief in Rosemary's eyes. 'Oliver! You haven't told Rosemary, have you? My God, you have. Why the hell couldn't you mind your own . . .'

Stephen sucked in his cheeks. What was the point of taking

his wrath out on Oliver? At the end of the day he'd obviously meant no harm. The person he needed to speak to was Rosemary. Aware of her cadaverous appearance, he took her gently by the arm and led her through a sea of happy, smiling faces to get her coat. There was some serious talking to do.

Taking a taxi back to the hotel, their stilted conversation centred mainly on day-to-day trivia and the party. Stephen also mentioned that he'd heard from Jake, who was offering Jane the chance to look round the theatre, chat to producers and staff, and also catch a matinée performance.

'I realize it could be a bit late as far as her dissertation is concerned,' he added, standing in the corridor outside their hotel room. 'Only it might help with some of her other projects.'

Rosemary watched him struggle with their keycard. 'I'm sure it will,' she replied, distant and aloof, at the same time highly relieved when the door eventually clicked open.

'Rosemary, please!' Stephen begged, helping her with the zip on her dress. 'For God's sake, say something. I know Oliver's told you about—'

'Your film assignment in America?'

'Look, I swear I was going to tell you, although you probably won't believe me. My intention had been to wait until after Oliver's party, when we were alone and had more time together.'

Rosemary said nothing. She was already struggling to keep control of her emotions.

Stephen paced the floor, clenching and unclenching his fingers. 'I'd already committed myself to the role before I met you,' he said, his tone desperate. 'At the time I couldn't wait for it to come round, couldn't wait to get away from England

and all those bloody photographers. Now . . .'

Struggling with the remaining few centimetres of zip, Rosemary let her dress fall silently to the floor. Her head swam and she turned to face him. 'And now?' she faltered, toying with the strap of her black lace basque.

'Now I can't even bear the thought of being parted from you. If only you knew how much I've dreaded this moment.'

'H-how long . . . How long will you be away?'

'Six months, maybe longer.'

Suppressing an anguished cry, Rosemary could only stare at him with sad, dull eyes. Six months. It had been bad enough not seeing him for six whole days.

'You know yourself what it's like,' Stephen said, fumbling with the pearls she'd left on the polished mahogany dressing table. 'Sometimes there's no control over these things. I was going to ask you to come with me. You know as well as I do that's totally impractical.'

Rosemary struggled for comprehension. What exactly did he mean?

'To begin with it would be grossly unfair to take you out to God knows where when I don't even know myself where I shall be living or what hours I shall be working. It's something that's never bothered me before, but I refuse to have you living in a caravan or some sleazy motel while I'm filming. Then there's Jane and Ben and also your parents to consider. Knowing you as I do, the last thing you'd want is to leave Jane in the middle of her finals, or your mother while she's waiting for a hip replacement. Am I right?'

Seeing her nod silently in reply, Stephen continued, 'Last but not least is your new book. I'm definitely not going to jeopardize your chances there. I thought that perhaps while I'm away you'd be able to finish it and even begin something new.'

Taking precious little comfort from his reasoning, whilst at the same time wondering what would happen if he found something new, Rosemary could only stammer 'Oh, Stephen, what if. . . ?'

Her sentence, however, remained unfinished. Walking purposefully towards her, Stephen's hands gripped her shoulders, his mouth and his tongue hungrily seeking hers. Moments later, when he lowered her roughly on to the bed, Rosemary forced her eyes shut as if trying to block from her mind his imminent departure. Clinging to him as their love-making became even more frenzied and intense, she felt as if her heart would break.

An hour later, with their tortured desires abated, neither of them spoke. Save for the sound of her shallow breathing, it was Stephen who eventually broke the silence in the unlit room.

'Rosemary we really have to discuss this.'

'I know, but I don't want to.'

Reaching into the darkness, Stephen drew her close. Physically he might have her in his arms; mentally it was as if she was slipping away from him completely. 'We must, if we're to consider a future together,' he struggled, the words choking in his throat. 'Can't you see how important it is? Because . . . I love you.'

To Rosemary at that moment it was no use, no use at all. Hearing the three words he'd never spoken before made any further talk impossible. She could only sob uncontrollably in his arms.

In the early morning light they parted, Stephen because he was expecting a call from the States and Rosemary because all she wanted to do was go home. She had the beginnings of a most dreadful headache.

'I'll ring you as soon as I know what's happening,' he assured her, cupping her face in his hands. 'Promise me you'll reconsider.'

Paralyzed with foreboding, Rosemary could only watch his retreating figure and succumb to yet more silent fears.

Half an hour later, and fresh from the shower that had done nothing to clear her throbbing temples, she became even more haunted by the vision of Stephen walking away from the hotel. How she longed for his presence. Yet it was all too late, she acknowledged grimly. Too late to tell him that he'd been right all along. Too late to apologize for her unforgivable bout of histrionics. All she could do now was make her way home.

'It's your own stupid fault. You've only got yourself to blame,' she told her hollow-eyed reflection in the mirror. 'If you'd had any sense at all you would have realized acting is his whole life.'

Stephen had to make a living just like anyone else, her inner self protested, as she gathered up her belongings. He'd spoken of the bad times often enough. And much as she would have done anything to assist him, she also knew he was far too proud and stubborn to accept any financial support from herself.

Convinced that even now he'd be regretting the fact that he'd ever set eyes on such a selfish woman, Rosemary straightened the crumpled bedclothes in search of her missing underwear. Why, oh why, had she overreacted? Clasping the basque and matching briefs to her breast, she already knew the answer. Not only had she loved him too much, but also deep in her heart, she'd been far too afraid to admit it. In truth, she'd never loved like this before and it hurt like hell.

Desperately flinging clothes into her suitcase, Rosemary

forced herself to think of anything other than Stephen's impassioned pleading. Silently mouthing some lines attributed to Robbie Burns, she began, '*Is there, in human form, that bears a heart, a wretch! a villain! lost to love and truth!*'

'And there's no greater wretch than you, Rosemary,' she muttered bitterly, stooping to pick up her dress, where it lay like a discarded corpse, drained of all life source. Wasn't that exactly how she felt? Shrivelled, numbed and emotionally drained at the prospect of a life without Stephen. With her head thumping even worse than before, she bundled the dress under her arm and moved to the dressing table. Wasn't that where she'd seen him fidgeting with her jewellery?

With her fevered mind in turmoil (Surely she couldn't be getting a migraine? She hadn't had one of those in years). Rosemary reached for the single row of pearls and earrings. To her horror they were no longer there. In their place was a cruel, twisted mouth, with two large opaque eyes staring back at her against the dark, polished furniture.

'Oh, Stephen!' she cried, pushing away the distorted shape. 'How can I possibly go on without you?'

Reminding herself of Jane's study timetable, Rosemary let herself into Laura's flat. She couldn't possibly face the train journey home just yet and with Jane in the middle of lectures, she would at least be spared any further embarrassing questions. To begin with Jane would want to know why her mother was looking so awful, never mind why she'd behaved like an overwrought schoolgirl.

Later, sponging her face with cold water and her head feeling marginally clearer, Rosemary contemplated ringing Stephen. Convinced he'd be at home, she even rehearsed an apology and explanation for her irrational outburst. Having spoken of their unhappy relationships in the past, was it expecting too much of him to comprehend why she feared the future?

Picking up the phone to dial his number, she quickly changed her mind. If Stephen was expecting that all-important call from America, he would want the line kept free. She must allow him that. Not knowing what to do next, she rummaged frantically in the bottom of her vanity case for a packet of mints (at least that should take away the sickening taste in her mouth), retrieving not only the small oblong box but also the two letters from Laura and Sarah, wedged between the pages of a writing pad. Her friends were still awaiting their replies, her original intention being to answer them while on the journey home.

Contemplating Stephen's imminent departure, Laura's offer grew more tempting than before. On the other hand, taking into account their acrimonious parting, it didn't necessarily follow that he would want her in the States any more. Besides, America was such a vast country and hadn't Stephen told her he hadn't a clue where he was going be on location?

Eventually conceding there was no harm in giving Laura a call, Rosemary was confronted with one of her pet hates. The answerphone. Her heart sank listening to Laura's message advising any caller that she was out of town, attending a publishing convention.

'*Please don't hang up*,' Laura's voice begged in her perfect Queen's English. '*I loathe these contraptions just as much as you. Leave your name and number and I'll get back to you as soon as I can.*'

Not wishing to ignore the plea, Rosemary left a brief and concise message. Her only chance now was Sarah but that could wait until later. If she didn't leave in the next five minutes she'd probably miss her train.

Relieved to be home in familiar surroundings, Rosemary
didn't know what to do first – put the kettle on for a welcoming cup of tea (she'd had nothing to eat or drink all day), take
some tablets for her splitting headache, or ring Stephen? To
her dismay, the first and second time she rang his line was
engaged and on the third attempt there was no reply. There
was now only one remaining option . . .

'Please be there. Please be there. Please . . .' Rosemary
mouthed in rhythm with each ringing tone. Ten minutes later
she scribbled notes to Jane and Ben and hunted for her book
of stamps. If she was quick, she might just catch the post on
the corner.

That errand completed, she returned to the house, threw
some clothes into a travel bag, filled the car with petrol and
set off for Sarah and Wales.

Stephen, meanwhile, paced the floor of his flat waiting for
his call from across the Atlantic, although when it eventually
came through he wasn't exactly in the mood for celebration.
Just as his agent had predicted, the offer was good, exceptionally good, in fact. What wasn't so good was the length of
the contract. It was for far longer than either of them had originally anticipated.

Hardly daring to complain – how could fate be so cruel? –
Stephen muttered his thanks and prepared to ring Rosemary.
Despite her protestations, it was only fair to tell her about the
duration of the contract. At least he owed her that. He didn't
want Oliver delivering that little bombshell as well.

'Damn you, Oliver!' he yelled, getting the constant engaged
tone and then no reply. 'If only you hadn't interfered we
could have had this whole thing sorted by now.'

Deciding he would try again later, he was beside himself with worry when he got no reply from Rosemary that day or the next. In desperation, his thoughts turned to Ben and Jane. They would certainly know where their mother was.

Remembering mother and daughter were so close and hoping perhaps Rosemary had gone to stay with Jane at the flat, his spirits lifted. Perhaps even now they would be having dinner together? He would go round immediately and use Jake and the Radclyffe play as an excuse.

Jane, surprised and delighted to see him, was in the middle of revision. To his acute dismay, there was no sign of Rosemary anywhere.

Motioning him to sit down, Jane moved a pile of files and books to free a space on the sofabed. 'Mum would have a fit if she saw this place now. As she's in Wales I suppose I am safe for the moment.'

'Wales?'

'Yes. Didn't you know? She's gone to stay with Sarah. Hey, you two haven't had a row or something?'

For the first time since he'd arrived, Jane noticed the dark circles under Stephen's eyes. It also looked as if he hadn't shaved for days. 'Oh my God, you have, haven't you?'

'I wouldn't exactly call it a row,' Stephen explained, his shoulders hunched. 'I'd prefer to call it a breakdown in communication.'

'Well, if there's anything I can do to help?'

'You could give me her phone number in Wales.'

'Of course, no problem. Now, where did I put Mum's note?' Turning aside assorted files and papers, Jane's search was in vain. 'Don't worry,' she added brightly, flicking through assorted textbooks, 'because I think I probably used it as a bookmark, or did I use the envelope for my shopping list

153

when I went to. . . ? Anyway, if all else fails and I can't find it,' Jane continued, hoping Stephen hadn't noticed the pile of used, soggy teabags on what could have been a shopping list and till receipt, 'I can always give you Sarah's name. The surname is Thomas and her husband's name is Haydn.'

'Jane,' Stephen groaned, burying his head in his hands, 'have you any idea exactly how many Haydn Thomases there must be in Wales?'

Chapter 12

Surprised by Rosemary's unexpected phone call, Sarah turned to face her husband.

'I don't understand it. Ro sounded so desperate on the phone. When I last spoke to her she said she was really looking forward to Oliver's party.'

Haydn eased off his boots and stretched out in front of the range. 'And I would have thought she'd be too tired to drive after all that partying in London.'

'Perhaps. But I'm still worried about her. It's not like Ro to drop everything like that. She always gives me at least a few days' notice.'

Haydn surveyed the chaos in the farmhouse kitchen. 'Ro's not expecting you to go dashing about with dusters and polish just because she's coming to stay for a bit.'

'No. Thank heavens,' Sarah sighed. 'But I would worry if it was her mother coming instead.'

Haydn reached out for his wife and drew her on to his lap, whispering in her ear, 'Lucky it isn't the old dragon then.'

Kissing his tanned and furrowed forehead, Sarah smiled adoringly into his deep brown eyes. 'Actually, I think the *old dragon* has mellowed over the years – at least since Gary died.'

'And not a moment too soon, eh? You don't think her father still blames me for Rosemary marrying Gary, do you?'

'Meaning that if you hadn't swept me off my feet all those years ago, and brought me here to the farm, I would have been there to warn Ro.'

'Warn? Gary wasn't a criminal, was he?'

'No, silly, although he did steal Ro's heart when she first met him. I'm afraid I shared Ro's dad's opinion of Gary. Neither of us were very keen on him – unlike the old dragon who thought her daughter had landed such a catch. Gary might have had pots of money but he was always so damned arrogant and had such shifty eyes.'

'Shifty eyes indeed.' Haydn grinned, aware that Sarah's eyes were filled with tears. 'Hey. What's up, love?'

'Oh, nothing. I'm just a sentimental old fool, thinking of the day you and I first met.'

Wrapped in her husband's embrace, Sarah was reminded of the holiday she and Rosemary had taken as teenagers. Straight from school, they'd decided on a camping holiday in Wales to celebrate the end of exams. Having spent the best part of a week bogged down by rain, they were in the process of going home when the weather changed. One clear blue sky had altered everything.

Sarah gave a languid sigh. The blue skies and billowing clouds outside the kitchen window were reminiscent of those as they'd stood on the battlements of Harlech Castle. Swept along by the romance of it all, the two girls had made a pact to remain friends for ever, discussed travelling to foreign lands to broaden their horizons and dreamt of tall and stately knights coming to their rescue.

Sarah's knight, however, had come in a completely different guise the very next day. Climbing the Roman Steps, she'd slipped and sprained her ankle. Unable to walk far, they'd stopped by a stream to bathe her swollen foot, only to be confronted by Haydn, looking for a lost lamb. Concerned and anxious to help, he'd bound Sarah's ankle with his handkerchief and carried his damsel in distress to flatter ground.

Haydn was neither tall nor stately. He was short and stocky with dark curly hair and eyes like pools of melted chocolate. What did it matter that he carried no sword or shield and that there was no trusty charger by his side? Seeing the tiny lamb slung round his neck and the scruffy sheepdog following on behind, Sarah was smitten. Who could fail to admire this gallant hero, set against the mountain backdrop with its fairy-tale scenery?

'That mountain looks so mystical and romantic,' she'd sighed, gazing dreamily into peat-brown eyes.

'Really?' Haydn had replied in his lilting, cheery voice. 'In that case, if you like it you can have it. It's mine and it's certainly no good for sheep.'

By Christmas and with school and exam results far behind them, Sarah and Haydn were married. In no time at all she found herself installed in a rambling stone farmhouse in Wales, ready to help her husband with his first batch of early lambs.

'So much for the secretarial sixth,' she whispered, suddenly reminded of Rosemary's imminent arrival.

Haydn's face filled with concern. This shabby, chaotic kitchen full of wellington boots and dogs was probably not what Sarah had envisaged married life to be. 'You don't regret it, do you, Sarah?'

'No! Of course not. Whatever gave you that idea?' She ran her hands through his thick, dark curls as if to reassure him. 'I love you so much. It's . . .'

'I know,' he murmured, taking her hand and kissing the tips of her fingers. 'Perhaps it's just as well Rosemary is coming then?'

Sarah's face brightened. 'Yes. Ro's exactly what I need at the moment. Now, where's our terrible trio? I don't think it would hurt them to come and help me clear this place up.'

Iwan, Gareth and Roanne responded to their mother's call, delighted with her change in countenance. Her mood of late had been strangely disconcerting. If Rosemary's visit was the reason for this new-found cheerfulness, they couldn't wait for her to arrive.

Anxious faces peered into the dusk for any sign of head-lights climbing the steep, winding track to the farm. Before too long, excited shrieks from the landing heralded Rosemary's arrival. Sarah, Haydn, children and dogs tumbled into the yard. The two women fell into each other's arms, crying.

'Oh, Ro. It's so good to see you,' Sarah cried. 'I've been wanting you to come for ages.'

'And I thought this was going to be a happy occasion,' Haydn teased, watching the two women wipe away their tears.

'It is,' Sarah sniffed, reaching out to pat Rosemary's head. 'Look at your hair. I know you told me you had it all cut off but I never imagined it would look so lovely. There you are, Roanne, see what I mean?'

The thirteen-year-old Roanne stood shyly, watching the two women hug each other. When Rosemary heard her goddaughter's name, she turned to embrace her.

'What's up, Roanne, darling? Has she been nagging you to have your lovely hair cut again?' Fingering the mass of curls that enveloped dark brown eyes in a pale oval face, Rosemary whispered with a grin, 'Ignore her. When your mother was your age, you should have seen what she did to her hair.'

Roanne turned and grinned at her mother, who realized daughter and godmother were already conspiring against her. Yet she also knew, with Ro looking so stunning, it wouldn't be long before Roanne followed suit and cut off her unruly locks. She only hoped this time she would have it done properly and not use her grandfather's sheep-shearing scissors!

With Rosemary freshening up after her journey and Iwan fetching her luggage from the car, the ever-observant Haydn concluded something was definitely up.

Sarah poured boiling water into a large earthenware teapot. 'You noticed it, too, then? It wasn't just my imagination?'

Haydn nodded, deeply thoughtful. 'In some ways she looks absolutely great, what with her new hairstyle and all. It's her eyes that upset me the most. They look haunted somehow . . . like an animal in pain.'

'There speaks a true farmer,' Sarah said, cutting thick wedges of fruit cake. 'Can you carry the tray through for me?'

Haydn stood behind his wife and placed his hands on the gentle curve of her stomach. 'You look tired, my love. Are you sure you're all right?'

Sarah nodded. 'I expect I'm like Ro. I'll be better after a good night's sleep. By the way no questions, eh? Let's just leave her and I'll try and find out what's wrong in the morning.'

The next day, after breakfast and with the children at school, Haydn gave his wife a knowing look and moved to the door. 'Right, you lovely ladies, I've work to do. I'll leave you to chat.'

Waving goodbye, Rosemary turned to see Sarah place a

coffee pot and two mugs on the kitchen table. 'He doesn't change, does he? Ever the considerate Haydn. You are so lucky.'

'I know and I absolutely adore him. Anyway, we don't want to talk about my man, do we? Aren't you going to tell me about yours?'

Rosemary's face filled with confusion. 'C'mon, Ro,' Sarah urged passing her a coffee. 'It is a man, isn't it? I mean, I've only got to look at you. New hairstyle, new clothes, the latest bootleg trousers and ankle boots. You look so different . . . it can only be a man.'

'Does it show that much?'

'Of course it does. It's written all over your face. Is it Oliver?'

For the first time in twenty-four hours, Rosemary laughed heartily. 'Good heavens, no!'

'In that case, I can only guess it's Stephen Walker, only I thought the two of you loathed each other? I know he took you to dinner ages ago and you haven't said much about him since.'

Without warning, Rosemary burst into floods of tears. When Haydn popped his head round the door, Sarah put a finger to her lips and motioned for him to leave. Alone again, she went to sit by her friend's side.

Calmed by the comforting sound of Sarah's voice and the enveloping warmth of the kitchen, Rosemary described her visit to Norfolk with Stephen.

This has to be serious, Sarah thought to herself. Ro rarely took people to the cottage. It was her own secret domain. Not wishing to pry, it was all so difficult knowing exactly where to begin. 'Did he . . . Did Stephen hurt you?' she asked eventually.

'What? No. He was wonderful. It was wonderful. He was so gentle and . . . Oh, what am I going to do, Sarah? I simply don't know how—'

'What don't you know?' Sarah encouraged gently.

'I don't know how to cope with it. Stephen made me feel like I've never felt before. So relaxed and warm and wanted. I've never been used to that. You know what Gary was like once we were married.'

Only too well, Sarah refrained from saying, convinced it was her fault Ro had married Gary. She stroked Ro's pale hands with her own well-worn red ones and reproached herself bitterly. Having been together since infant school, she and Ro were like sisters. She should never have allowed Ro to marry Gary Fielding. Such an arrogant bastard he was, looking down on Haydn's family and their farm!

'I'm sorry, Ro. If only I hadn't been so far away, you might never have married Gary.'

Rosemary reached for a handkerchief and blew her nose. 'You know,' she sniffed, 'I only discovered recently that on the morning of my wedding my father actually cried. He thought I was making a big mistake, but Mother—'

'We all knew what your mother thought. Gary Fielding, the bee's knees at Farmer and Butler, with such excellent prospects. I can hear her now.'

'In a way they were both right. Gary was a very astute businessman and certainly took care of all our material needs.'

'Hmph! And what about your emotional ones? From what little you've told me, it certainly sounds as if Stephen Walker's been seeing to those.'

Rosemary blushed, sipping at her coffee. 'If I hadn't married Gary I suppose I would never have met Stephen. What am I going to do, Sarah? The problem is I love him so much.'

Sarah laughed. 'There was me thinking I was the simple country girl and all along it's you being a goose! If you really love him, Ro, surely there isn't any problem?'

Tears welled once more in Rosemary's eyes. 'You d-don't understand,' she faltered. 'Stephen's going away to America and I simply can't imagine life without him.'

'Why not tell him how you feel and if he loves you—'

'That's just it. I can't tell him now. We've had a row.'

'You mean a proper row, like the real humdingers my parents used to have?'

'No,' Rosemary replied, reminded of Sarah's parents yelling and screaming at each other. 'But I did behave like a complete idiot when Stephen first told me he was going away. I can't believe how stupid I was. I wouldn't even listen to him – let alone talk to him. Besides,' she added as an afterthought, 'he's seven years younger than me. What will people think?'

'To hell with what people think! Anyway, what's seven years? You certainly don't look your age. At least you didn't until you started making your eyes all red and puffy.'

Forcing a weak smile, Rosemary reached for another tissue and dried her eyes. Sarah patted her hand. 'That's better. Please don't cry any more. So . . . tell me, has Stephen ever said anything about the age difference?'

'Not much. He says he's never noticed.'

'Ro Fielding! What am I going to do with you?'

'What do you mean?'

'If Stephen's not bothered about it, why the hell should you?'

'Because of the future. I couldn't bear to be hurt again. Not only that, where's it all going to end?'

'End? Good grief! By the sounds of it you two have only

162

just begun. Let's not talk about endings. And if Stephen's as good and kind as you say, he wouldn't want to see you hurt.'

'Do you honestly believe that?' Rosemary replied, collecting the empty mugs and taking them to the sink.

'Course I do. Anyway, we all do stupid things, you know – even me.'

Rosemary turned a quizzical eye in her direction. 'You?'

'I'm pregnant, Ro.'

When Rosemary opened her mouth to speak, nothing came out.

'Exactly,' Sarah nodded, her face taking on a grave appearance. 'My turn to cry on your shoulder, I think.'

For what seemed like an eternity the two women hugged each other in silence. 'Are you sure?' Rosemary said at length, her eyes scanning Sarah's stomach hidden beneath one of Haydn's rugby shirts. 'Have you thought it could be your age? We must both be heading towards the menopause.'

'You might be, Ro. As for me, I'm heading for the nearest maternity hospital. Even the doctor couldn't believe it, especially after the problems I had conceiving the first three. I might have been married first but you were the one who had no trouble getting pregnant. Do you know, before my pregnancy test, the doctor was about to suggest a course of HRT.'

'Hmm. If you ask me, you've already had it. Aren't they Haydn's initials?'

Sarah's face creased into ripples of laughter. 'So they are,' she cried. 'Haydn Richard Thomas.'

Highly delighted by the scene that met his eyes when he appeared for elevenses, Haydn heard his wife remark, 'Ro Fielding, you are exactly what the doctor ordered. Now, while I feed this Welsh ram of mine, promise me you'll ring Stephen and tell him how you feel.'

Determined to make things right between them, Rosemary hurried to the phone. Even if she couldn't see Stephen for a few days (she'd already decided Sarah and Haydn obviously needed her support), she would at least have a chance to apologize and explain her innermost fears. He loved her, didn't he? Sarah had convinced her of that. In which case he was bound to understand.

Ten minutes passed before Rosemary returned to the kitchen. 'He wasn't there,' she said dejectedly, in response to Sarah's questioning gaze. 'I'll try again later.'

Later that day and the next there was still no reply, until she gave up ringing altogether. It was only when she rang Jane towards the end of the week that she discovered Stephen's whereabouts.

'He's staying with Jake De Havilland for the next few days until he goes to the States,' Jane announced matter-of-factly.

'The next few days?' Rosemary gasped. 'You mean he's already booked to go?'

'So it would seem. Stephen told me only last night, his agent's got everything sorted and there's little point in hanging around.'

Wondering why Stephen should have been at Jane's and also trying to digest his 'little point in hanging round', Rosemary struggled for something to say. It was no good; the words simply stuck in her throat.

'Of course it would have been better if you and Stephen could have resolved your differences before he went,' Jane said, half-listening to her mother, half-looking through the pages of an essay, while juggling the phone and a cup of coffee. 'I don't know why you haven't rung him.'

'Haven't rung him? I've rung him morning, noon and night. The trouble is Stephen's like me, he loathes answerphones and mobiles. He's also never at home.'

'Course he isn't,' Jane said, knowledgeably. 'During the day he's been finalizing things with his agent, visiting his family in Sheffield or spending time with Jake, except when there's been a matinée. In the evenings . . . Oh, bum! Hang on a minute. I've just dropped my essay and there's pages everywhere.'

'The evenings', Rosemary repeated to herself, reminded of the wonderful evenings she'd spent locked in Stephen's arms. This past week she had been spending her evenings with Sarah and Haydn. But what of Stephen? Where had he been spending his?

'Right. I think I've got them all,' Jane said, out of breath. 'Now, where was I?'

'Er – telling me about Stephen's evenings.'

'Oh, yes. Well, he's spent most of those here with me, drowning his sorrows. Can you believe he actually complimented me on my cooking? And he's been a terrific help with some of my essays. Not only that, he's suggested meeting him for a farewell lunch tomorrow, then he's taking me to see Jake De Havilland. I'm hoping for a tour of the theatre. Stephen was saying . . .'

A farewell lunch? Rosemary wanted to cry out. It all sounded so final. Was this the end then, as far as she and Stephen were concerned? 'D-didn't he say anything about me?' she whispered, attempting indifference.

There was a rustle of papers before Jane replied. 'What? No, not really, other than that he thought what you need at the moment is plenty of rest and Welsh mountain air to clear your head. Although I suppose it might have been easier if he'd had Sarah's number earlier.'

'But I gave you Sarah's number. Couldn't you have given it to him?'

Jane remembered the hunt for Rosemary's letter. Too embarrassed to tell her mother the envelope had ended up under a pile of soggy teabags, and the hastily written note had turned up at the bottom of her bed days later, she said quickly, 'I know, Mum. But you know what this place is like when exams are looming. Anyway, it wasn't a problem cos I rang Ben and got it from him – lucky I caught him as he was just going out. Unfortunately, by the time we'd finished supper we decided it was too late to ring. Stephen and I are both night owls, don't forget, whereas Sarah and Haydn get up with the first cock crow. Then, when Stephen did try ringing you, he discovered Ben had given me the wrong number. Duh! That's Ben for you.'

Grateful that Jane had at last paused for breath, Rosemary began to wonder if this was all part of some horrid conspiracy. A deliberate plot to keep herself and Stephen apart. In her present frame of mind (and with her head beginning to ache again), she was beginning to wonder if she'd given birth to two complete imbeciles.

When the dull pounding in her head appeared to coincide with Jane dropping the handset of the phone, Rosemary was on the point of despair. Moments later, with much rustling and cursing and the instantly recognizable sound of a distant coffee mug crashing to the floor, followed by Jane's subsequent cry, 'Oh, shit. All over my bloody essay!', Rosemary hung up the phone.

'Welsh mountain air and plenty of rest,' Rosemary repeated to herself time and time again in the weeks following Stephen's hasty departure from England.

The first came in abundance, the latter wasn't quite so easy. Jane's surprise announcement that Stephen had phoned with news of a proposed visit to the UK was made on the very same day Rosemary was at the hospital with Sarah. Sarah's scan showed she was expecting twins.

Determined to hide her disappointment that it was Jane Stephen appeared to be confiding in, Rosemary mustered a smile.

'Stephen might not want me any more, but you certainly do,' she said, stroking Sarah's forehead as she lay in bed, trying to come to terms with the previous day's shock announcement. Even Haydn's usual ruddy and weather-beaten face was deathly pale and his eyes lacklustre.

'What are we going to do, Sarah?' he asked, trying to conceal his fear and anxieties. Roanne's birth had been so difficult that the doctor had even warned of the dangers for further pregnancies.

Rosemary, meanwhile, forced Stephen to the back of her mind. Rearranging Sarah's pillows, she answered on her friend's behalf. 'Do?' she replied confidently. 'I would have thought that was obvious.'

Sarah and Haydn fixed her with vacant stares.

'You really can't see, can you? And there was me thinking you were sheep farmers.'

'We are,' they replied lamely.

'Then think of it from a farming point of view – which is sheep.'

'Sheep?' Haydn's mouth gaped open.

'Exactly.' Rosemary grinned. 'Those fluffy white things on four thin black legs.'

'Ro,' Sarah said feebly, 'I'm sorry. You'll have to excuse us. Wonderful though it is to see you smiling for once, I don't think either of us are in the mood for your sense of humour today.'

'No. Of course not. Sorry. I should have realized. What I'm trying to say is that like a sheep having two lambs and not one, it's a bonus. Sarah, my dear. Can't you see? To me your babies are going to be twin lambs and I intend to stay here as your shepherdess until they're born.'

'Our what? Ro, are you mad? You can't possibly stay here and look after me until the babies are born. What about your house and family?'

'Perhaps I'll go back and check on the house. As for the family, shall we just say they seem perfectly capable of taking care of themselves?'

Sarah regarded her husband. Had he also discerned a faintly acerbic tone in Ro's voice? 'That's all very well,' she began. 'But what about your new book?'

'No problem. I'll fetch my laptop and—'

'As far as I'm concerned there's no need to continue,' Haydn interrupted. 'I'm not sure about my lovely wife here, but I'm already persuaded. I'd feel a great deal happier knowing it's you who's keeping an eye on Sarah. Are you really sure?'

'Of course I am,' Rosemary lied convincingly, when she would have given anything to go to London in the hope of being there when Stephen returned.

'There'll be so much to do,' Sarah remonstrated, propping herself up on one elbow. 'I can't possibly expect you to—'

Rosemary held up her hand. 'And I shan't expect you to do anything except trust me. I'll cope admirably.'

'Liar!' she told herself several weeks later, when reminded of this conversation. Oh, yes, she'd coped up to a point. With so much to do all the time at least it numbed the pain and hurt inside whenever she thought of Stephen. When the sun shone in a clear blue sky, casting its golden glow across the fields and mountain tops, she was even at peace with the world. When it rained, however (and it had almost every day this week), her heart ached so much that the water cascading in rivulets down the sombre, grey slabs of mountain only mirrored the silent tears she was shedding within.

Chapter 13

Trying to remain cool and detached when Roanne came running in with the post containing Stephen's hastily written postcard, Rosemary was less in control when he phoned.

'Rosemary. At last! It's so good to hear your voice. I can't believe how difficult it's been trying to get hold of you.'

'I'm sorry. I did try ringing before you left. You never seemed to be at home.'

'So I understand. Jane told me you'd had problems locating me. And every time I tried ringing the farm you were out with Sarah or the children. One of the many disadvantages of being in a different time zone. Did you receive my postcard?'

'Yes. Thank you. The children were very impressed with the scenery.'

'I wish I was,' Stephen said, half-joking. 'I admit Death Valley is a pretty spectacular place to look at but filming has been a nightmare owing to the heat. Oh, to be back in wet and drizzly London. Which reminds me, did you know we practically took the flat apart hunting for your letter? How it ended up in Jane's bed I'll never know.'

Rosemary said nothing, preferring not to think of Stephen and Jane alone together in the flat. Particularly in the vicinity of Jane's bed.

Stephen gave a knowing laugh. 'Then when Ben couldn't find your letter either and tried to remember the number from memory . . .'

'That's hardly surprising,' Rosemary said, remembering her last visit to the student halls of residence. 'Ben's room is even worse than Jane's.'

'Anyway, enough about that. You still haven't told me how you are.'

'Oh, I'm fine.'

'And Sarah?'

'Much better now that she's over morning sickness. Did you hear about the scan?'

'Yes. Jane told me. Apparently, I'd been trying to ring you at the same time you were at the hospital with Sarah. Jane said the result came as quite a shock.'

Rosemary shuddered, thinking of the shock to her own system every time Stephen mentioned her daughter's name.

'So, am I going to see you?'

'See me?'

'When I come over to London. It appears the gods have been trying to keep us apart. Will you be able to leave Sarah and Haydn for a while? Only Jane was suggesting . . .'

From where Rosemary was standing it wasn't the gods who were keeping them apart, it was someone far less ethereal. Although if her memory served her correctly wasn't there a Roman god Janus? 'Well, Sarah has assured me she's OK now. She and Haydn are forever nagging me to go home and check on my own house and garden.'

'Wonderful. Perhaps you can check on me too? It will be great to see you again. You have absolutely no idea how awful I felt leaving as I did. We never got a chance to say a proper goodbye, did we?'

Stephen's words reverberated in Rosemary's head as she helped Sarah prepare the children's tea. What exactly had he meant by them? Deeply perplexed, she found herself making a mental list. Was it simply that they hadn't been able to say goodbye because a) he'd had to leave in a hurry, b) because she'd foolishly taken herself off to Wales? or c) what he'd really intended as a proper goodbye was something more permanent? As in: '*Goodbye, Rosemary, and thanks. It's been great knowing you. Now that I'm making a name for myself in America I'll be looking for someone younger.*'

Turning to someone younger herself, Rosemary offered to help Roanne with her homework.

'We're doing a project on Roman gods,' Roanne said, reaching for her textbook.

'How strange,' Rosemary reflected. 'I was thinking about a Roman god only this morning. At least I think he was Roman. Although . . . he could have been Greek.'

'Which one?'

'Janus.'

'He's definitely Roman,' Roanne announced proudly, tugging at her now much shorter curls. 'He's the god of beginning and endings.'

'Stop showing off,' her brother teased from across the table.

'I'm not. I only remembered cos my teacher said Janus has got two faces. Mr Williams says that's what he needs – especially when he's taking 4B. Then he can look in two directions at once.'

'Then he'd be just like Mum,' Gareth quipped. 'She's always saying she's got eyes in the back of her head.'

Having said goodnight to the children, Rosemary flicked absently through the pages of Roanne's book. Sure enough, there was a picture of Janus with two heads accompanied by the following text: '*To call someone Janus-faced is to describe them as two-faced and deceitful.*'

Beginnings, endings and deceit, Rosemary repeated in her head, and filled with a deep sense of foreboding, slammed the book shut. Knowing she would be seeing her very own Janus before too long, she wondered in which direction he would be facing.

Preparing to leave for home, Rosemary felt herself torn apart. Filled with sadness at leaving Sarah and Wales, she was also filled with nervous anticipation at the thought of meeting up with Stephen. That's if he was still in London? She sighed resignedly. Yet again, according to Jane, he was.

Trying to dismiss such painful thoughts from her mind, she reached for Roanne and held her tightly. 'I've asked Mummy if you can come and stay with me,' she whispered. 'I thought you might like to go shopping in London.'

Knowing her two older brothers wouldn't be at all interested in shopping, Roanne's face lit up at the prospect. She kissed her godmother goodbye and stepped back. It was time for her father to say his own farewells.

'Be happy, Rosemary,' Haydn said quietly, enveloping her in something akin to a rugby hold. 'Remember we're always here if you need us.'

With tears in her eyes, Sarah held out her arms. 'Oh, Ro. I shall really miss you. Thanks so much for all your help. I don't know what we'd have done without you. Now, remember what I said when you first arrived. Just let things happen. It *will* work out once you've had a chance to speak to Stephen. I promise.'

Will it? Rosemary questioned silently, opening the car door.

Somehow in recent months, she'd begun to lose all faith in promises.

Sarah stood with her hands resting on her visibly swollen stomach. 'Don't forget to ring me as soon as you've sorted things out with Stephen.'

'Only if you promise to ring me the moment the lambs' heads are engaged and I'll hotfoot it back to Wales immediately.'

'I promise.' Sarah grinned, when Haydn lovingly patted his wife's double bump.

Choking back a sob, Rosemary drove away, stopping only briefly for one last lingering glimpse in her rear-view mirror. Behind her were five tiny specks silhouetted against a backdrop of green hills and cornflower-blue skies, while ahead lay . . .

'Oh, Stephen,' she murmured, her white-knuckled hands gripping the steering wheel. The mere mention of his name was enough to cause her stomach to lurch.

In recent weeks she'd thought of him constantly whenever she was alone. Walking the hills while Sarah rested, she'd wanted nothing more than to feel the gentle touch of his lips on hers, see the soft breeze rustle his hair and catch the shimmering sunlight, dancing in his slate-grey eyes. Eyes the colour of the magnificent Welsh mountains that surrounded her on every side.

Turning the key in the lock, Rosemary opened her front door. Astonished by the almost immediate ringing of the phone, she ran to answer it. Her heart beating in expectation, it was Jane not Stephen who called excitedly down the phone.

'Mum! At last. Where have you been? We thought you were coming home days ago.'

'I was but Sarah was due for another antenatal check-up. I decided to go with her, just in case. I wanted to make sure everything was OK before I—'

'Trust you to be so thoughtful,' Jane interrupted. 'Good old Mum, what would we all do without you? I was only saying to Stephen, it feels as if you've been away for simply ages. We were beginning to wonder if you were ever coming back.'

'We?'

'Stephen, Ben and myself. Last night . . . we all got together for dinner at the flat. It was a real hoot. Oh, and you'll never guess what's happened.'

'Probably not.'

'Course you won't. The trouble with you is that you've been in the sticks for far too long. Seems whenever Stephen or I rang, you were always out wandering the fields like a hermit – or else helping Sarah and Haydn with their flock of both the four- and two-legged variety.'

'I don't know about wandering the fields like a hermit,' Rosemary protested, convinced that neither her daughter nor Stephen had rung as often as she claimed. 'But I was certainly kept very busy. Helping to run a farm, care for Sarah and look after three children can be pretty exhausting.'

'Exactly. Which is why I told Stephen that you'd probably prefer to be left in peace for a bit. Anyway, that's one of the reasons I'm ringing. Like I said, Stephen was here last night. In fact, he's been here most nights since he returned from the States. Of course, this is only a flying visit and he'll have to go back soon but—'

Rosemary groaned audibly. Stephen was already talking of returning to America?

'Mum, are you OK? You sound dreadful. Almost as bad as Stephen when he had jet lag. In your case, and what with you returning from Wales, should it be sheep lag?'

Jane waited, expecting her mother to laugh. When no response was forthcoming, she gave a quick shrug of the shoulders and continued unperturbed. 'As I was saying . . . About Stephen . . . he wants to take us all out for lunch. Can you make it tomorrow? Ben's coming too, he's on exam leave. I suggested The Orchard Bowl on the top floor next to the furniture department at . . .'

Reluctantly, Rosemary found herself agreeing if only to still Jane's excited chatter. She wanted so much to see Stephen again. But a reunion with Jane and Ben in tow? That wasn't quite how she'd visualized it during her long, lonely nights at the farm. With myriad thoughts of Wales, Roman gods and the recent conversation she'd had with Stephen spiralling out of control, she reached into the bathroom cabinet for some paracetamol. Not surprisingly, she felt a migraine coming on.

Wet and drizzly. Wasn't that how Stephen had described London? Hardly, Rosemary thought, shifting uncomfortably in her seat. In fact, it was anything but. The journey to London on a hot and humid summer's day was beset with problems she could well do without. Signal failures and works on the line she could just about cope with. This persistent migraine, however, was something else. With both tempers and temperatures in the stuffy, crowded compartment becoming even more heated, the thumping in her head grew steadily worse. If only she could close her eyes and sleep.

When the train eventually pulled into Euston, Rosemary rubbed at her throbbing temples and remained seated. Far better to stay put and avoid being crushed. Particularly if it meant avoiding the overbearing, power-dressed female wielding a copy of a well-known glossy magazine, pushing and shoving her way through the crowd.

In bemused silence, Rosemary left the train conscious of a sudden confrontation up ahead. From out of nowhere an unshaven, spotty-faced youth grabbed the offending magazine and prepared to toss it into a nearby bin.

'Nah!' he said, at Rosemary's approach. 'I expect that stupid cow 'ad only just bought it. 'Ere y'are, darlin'. You 'ave it. At least you look as if you'd read it instead of usin' it as a bleedin' weapon.'

Startled, Rosemary found herself holding the rolled-up magazine with its so-called celebrity couple adorning the front cover. Did she really want to read about yet another footballer? Deciding she didn't, she made her way to the nearest waste bin already filled to overflowing with rubbish.

Releasing her grasp on the magazine, Rosemary watched fascinated as a kaleidoscope of pages unfurled like a coiled spring. 'Goal,' she whispered, seeing both footballer and spouse covered in Coke tins and crisp packets. They didn't appear quite so glamorous now . . . and how strange that one of the other couples flickering by looked amazingly like . . . Stephen and Jane!

Transfixed with horror, Rosemary reached down and tore frantically at the inside feature pages of the magazine. She had to be mistaken. How could it possibly have been a photo of Stephen and Jane?

Don't be so ridiculous! a voice echoed in her head. *You're letting your imagination get the better of you. You should know by now what you're like when you get a migraine. You always . . .*

Attempting to steady herself, Rosemary felt suddenly sick, all colour draining from her face. Smoothing out a crumpled page, she studied two familiar figures, unexpectedly caught on camera leaving a top London jewellers.

Stephen, with his 'I hate the press. Why don't you leave me alone?' expression on his face, she recognized immediately. As for his pretty companion, clinging limpet-like on to his arm . . What could she say? Her daughter Jane was positively beaming.

Moving to a nearby bench while the crowds gradually drifted away, Rosemary sat with unseeing eyes and held the torn page against her breast. Jagged black lines appeared to flash across her temples and the feeling of nausea continued to engulf her.

'I knew I shouldn't have come,' she whispered, bile rising in her throat.

'But they're expecting you, Rosemary,' her other self sneered as she slipped the torn photo in her pocket. *'Didn't Jane say she and Stephen have so much to tell you? You'd better not be late.'*

In stark contrast to the openness and freedom of the Welsh hills with their clean and invigorating air, Rosemary found herself swept along airless corridors, bustled down stairs and jostled on to a crowded tube train. Hardly able to breathe, she stared about her in panic. Only three more stops. Please God she didn't pass out. Why hadn't she taken a taxi?

To her dismay, there was little relief at street level. Only a cacophony of noise and mayhem and a news vendor yelling in her ear. With dust and exhaust fumes choking the air, Rosemary longed for Wales, the farm and familiar smiling faces. 'Oh, Sarah,' she cried in desperation. 'What am I doing here?'

'Oi. You all right, luv? You want to watch yourself. You nearly ended up under that bus.'

Clasping a print-blackened hand, Rosemary waited until her eyes grew more accustomed to the dazzling sunlight. 'Thank you. Yes. I felt a bit dizzy, that's all. I – er – didn't have any breakfast.'

The man with almost as many lines on his face as the papers he was selling tut-tutted and shook his head. 'Just like my daughter, you are. She never 'as time for breakfast. The missus is always tellin' her orf about it. As for me, I always 'ave the works. Sausage, egg, bacon, fried bread and black pudding, all washed down with a nice mug of tea. Bloomin' luvverly that is. Tell you what ducks, that's probably what you need right now. A nice cuppa and a bite to eat. Why not pop over the road?'

Thinking how ironic, Jane and Stephen would be giving her the 'works' of the non-edible variety, Rosemary followed the news vendor's gaze to the department store opposite. It was where she was heading anyway. 'Yes, I will. I'll go right away,' she said, clasping her hand to her mouth.

Thanking him for his help, she bought a paper, glancing only briefly at the headlines. Something about the ongoing heatwave, summer storms and yet more serious fires burning out of control.

'Thank Gawd I ain't a fireman,' he said, folding another paper. 'Now don't forget to have something to eat, luv. By the looks of you I'd say you're not the all-day breakfast type at all. But they do say The Fruit Dish is very nice.'

With a half-hearted smile, Rosemary crossed the road. In a way, he was almost right. What he probably meant to say was The Orchard Bowl. That's where she was supposed to be meeting Jane.

Relieved to find the temperature inside the store considerably cooler, Rosemary stopped by the perfume counter. Anxious to get her bearings, she also willed the jagged black lines, still darting angrily in front of her eyes, to go away.

Go? Go where? she puzzled. Where was she supposed to go? Surely not up there, where endless steel jaws snaked their way ever higher. All those people. All those lumbering pairs of feet and strident voices going up . . . and up . . . and up.

Anxious to escape a cloud of sickly sweet perfume, Rosemary stepped forward, clasped the moving handrail, and then quickly changed her mind. It was no good. Going one floor on the escalator was bad enough, going all the way to the top was completely out of the question. There had to be another way.

Reminded that not since Gary's aneurysm had she had such a dreadful attack of migraine, Rosemary side-stepped the escalators and peered at her watch. She was late anyway. Wasn't it safer to use the stairs?

Safer in more ways than one, she concluded bitterly, trembling fingers reaching for the banister rail. This way at least she'd have more time to think. How many steps to climb? How many metres of handrail to hold? How many minutes until she reached the top floor? And then the most difficult question of them all. What would she say to Stephen and Jane? Only when the smell of freshly squeezed orange juice assailed her nostrils, followed by the unmistakable sound of her daughter's laughter, did she stop counting.

Taking a deep breath, Rosemary came to a halt at the top of the stairs. Stephen and Jane she noticed, were sitting alone at a table in the far corner. Unaware of her presence Stephen cast a furtive look towards the escalator, whispered something to Jane and reached in the pocket of his jacket. The blue jacket. The same blue jacket he wore on our first date, Rosemary recollected, memories of that wonderful night flooding back.

Horror struck, she watched her daughter's face radiate into a smile when Stephen placed a small box on the table. Examining its contents, Jane's eyes shone with happiness until all at once – and as if checking to see the coast was clear

– she looked about her, clasped his hand and . . . kissed him! Choking back tears, Rosemary wanted to run. How could they do this to her? No wonder Stephen was desperate to see her. No wonder Jane had sounded so excited on the phone.

Anxious not to draw attention to herself, Rosemary hid behind a pillar. Had Stephen ever loved her, she wondered, or had he simply been using her once he'd been introduced to Jane? Jane, who was forever saying she wasn't at all attracted to men with blond hair (she much preferred the likes of Fergus Buchanan and Jake De Havilland), while all the time, and behind her mother's back, she'd been entertaining Stephen at the flat.

Hurriedly slipping away to the cloakroom, Rosemary bathed her eyes with cool water and fumbled in her handbag for a pair of sunglasses.

'Well, Stephen Walker,' she muttered with grim determination, 'you might pride yourself on being a pretty good actor. Here's where I show you I can deliver an equally impressive performance.'

Seeing her approach, Stephen hurriedly removed the tiny ring box to his pocket. He stood up, guilt and anxiety written all over his face.

'Rosemary. We've been so worried about you. We thought something dreadful had happened.'

Watching Stephen embrace her mother and help her to a chair, Jane looked on, concerned. 'Mummy, darling. Why the Greta Garbo? Gracious, you're as white as a sheet. Are you sick?'

The words 'sick with betrayal' sprang to mind but were swallowed immediately with a mouthful of bile. Instead Rosemary forced a nonchalant reply. 'I'm fine, thank you, but would you believe it? After all these years without them, I've got one of those awful migraines. It must be the change of air. The journey to London was an absolute nightmare.'

'Oh, dear. Poor you. And such a shame because you've missed Ben. He said he was sorry he couldn't wait any longer and I'm afraid I've already eaten. Stephen hasn't, though. He wanted to wait for you. Isn't that sweet?'

'What? Oh, yes. Very,' Rosemary replied, the pounding in her head reaching stereo point.

'Well, here's where I love you and leave you – important things to do,' Jane grinned slyly, giving Stephen a conspiratorial look.

Taking Jane's hand Stephen leaned forward to kiss her cheek. Never one for whispering quietly, Jane's *'Good luck, Stephen. Break it to her gently. Don't forget we've already got Gran and Grandad's approval and that Ben also thinks it's cool'* echoed cruelly across the table.

Watching her go, Stephen turned to Rosemary and shook his head. 'That daughter of yours is simply amazing, isn't she? I expect she's already told you the reason for this unexpected but extremely welcome trip. Who'd have thought it, eh? Oliver doesn't exactly share in our enthusiasm, of course. In fact, he's had more than a few words to say on the subject.'

With a brittle smile Rosemary pretended to study the menu. At least she still had an ally in Oliver. 'Stephen,' she said eventually. 'Would you mind? I'm not at all hungry. In fact, as my headache appears to be getting worse than ever, I think I'd rather leave.'

'Leave?' Stephen rose from his chair to help her. 'What an idiot I am,' he said, placing an arm about her shoulders. 'Here I am chattering merrily away about my good fortune when it's obvious you're not feeling at all well. Perhaps you should go to bed?'

Rosemary froze when Stephen hailed a taxi and gave the address of his flat. He couldn't possibly expect her to go back with him after the scene she'd just witnessed in the restaurant.

'I think I'd prefer to go to Jane's,' she said hurriedly. 'At least it's only round the corner from Euston. I can go home as soon as I've rested.' She refrained from adding that at least there she could go to bed alone.

Outside the entrance now familiar to them both, Stephen took her hand.

'Rosemary – um – if you haven't already guessed, there's something really important I need to talk to you about. Not now, of course, as it wouldn't be fair. I can see you're not up to it.' Shifting uneasily, unable to see her reaction behind her dark glasses, Stephen resumed. 'You know, Jane's right. You do look quite dreadful. Why not have a good night's sleep and I'll ring you first thing tomorrow. Regrettably, I didn't realize you would be staying quite so long in Wales. I'm taking Ben to a European cup match this evening. However, Jane did suggest I ask you . . . and I was also, er, wondering . . . are you by any chance planning to go to the cottage this weekend?'

Rosemary was aghast. The cottage. Why should he want to know about the cottage? What exactly were Jane and Stephen planning together?

Though still not feeling one hundred per cent, Rosemary prepared to leave the flat, only to come face to face with her daughter.

'Mum? What are you doing?'

'I was just leaving.'

'Leaving? Leaving for where?'

'To catch my train.'

Jane studied her mother's ghostly pallor. 'Catch a train? You've got to be joking. The only place you're going is bed. If you don't mind my saying so, you look absolutely bloody awful!'

'Thanks. As if I needed reminding,' Rosemary muttered, glimpsing her reflection in the hall mirror.

Insisting that Rosemary undress, Jane quickly rearranged the unmade bed and drew the curtains. 'There. Bed. Sleep and a darkened room. That's what you need. What about tablets?'

Rosemary pointed to the wastepaper basket and the empty pink box. She'd already taken the maximum dose.

'Hmph!' Jane snorted. 'Looks like it's just as well I came back. Having swallowed that little lot you'd probably have ended up jumping in front of the train, not getting on it.'

Perhaps I should, Rosemary thought to herself, watching her daughter head in the direction of the bathroom.

Turning on the shower, Jane stripped to her bra and pants and came running back into the bedroom. Rosemary was deeply envious. Jane had mentioned she'd been working out at a gym. It showed. There was not an inch of cellulite anywhere. No wonder Stephen . . .

'Now off to sleep with you,' Jane said, snatching pretty lace undies from a drawer. 'I'm going out anyway and I promise not to wake you when I come back. Promise me you'll stay there and I'll bring you breakfast in bed in the morning. Not the bacon and egg thing – Stephen says I'm useless at that – but I can just about manage tea and toast.'

Rosemary clutched at her mouth. The very mention of food—

Twenty minutes later, when Jane tiptoed into the bedroom, Rosemary was dozing fitfully. 'Just going, Mum. Catch up with all the news soon. Oh, and by the way, I bought you a magazine. It's in the kitchen.' Pausing by the door, Jane whispered into the darkness. 'Have a look at page a hundred and nineteen. I'm dying to know what you think.'

Waking several hours later, Rosemary struggled unsteadily to her feet. At least she wasn't feeling quite so queasy and the hammering in her head had ceased. Dare she risk a cup of tea? Deciding she would, she looked at her watch and made her way to the bathroom. It was pointless getting dressed. She would borrow a bathrobe instead. As long as it wasn't saturated in Jane's usually cloying and exceedingly sickly perfume.

Pleased to discover Jane had changed her perfume to an unusual and subtle blend of citrus and musk, Rosemary adjusted the sash of the bathrobe, walked back to the kitchen and filled the kettle. Now all she had to do was find a clean cup.

'What a mess,' she said, her gaze taking in the pile of dirty crockery, empty food packets, discarded clothing and textbooks. 'Jane, dear. As your gran is forever telling you, you'll make a terrible . . .'

The word wife froze on Rosemary's lips. On the work surface in front of her was a copy of the latest *Brides* magazine.

Hardly daring to look, Rosemary picked up the magazine and struggled to recall her daughter's farewell message. What was it? Something about page nineteen and let me know what you think?

Turning the pages she saw page number nineteen contained nothing more than an advertisement for a very expensive face cream. How bizarre. Jane was hardly the type to get excited over a jar of face cream. Assuming she'd got the wrong page, it must be one hundred and nineteen, Rosemary flicked ahead through page after page of fresh-faced girls in swirls of tulle and lace. One hundred and seventeen . . . one hundred and eighteen . . . one hundred and nineteen. So, she had been right all along. The words, in bold black print, jumped out to greet her: 'Mother of the Bride – the Latest High-Street Fashions.'

Through her own veil of tears, not tulle, Rosemary ran to the bedroom and fumbled in her jacket pocket for a handkerchief, even more distraught to discover the crumpled photo she'd torn from the magazine at Euston. She simply couldn't believe it. After all this time, when mother and daughter had always seemed so close, how could Jane be so cruel?

Chapter 14

Early next morning Jane knocked gently on the bedroom door, placed a tray of tea and toast on the side table and, pleased to see her mother looking better, announced she was going to the library. 'I expect you'll be gone by the time I get back, so have a safe journey home and a super weekend.' She plumped up Rosemary's pillows and examined the contents of the breakfast tray. 'Is there anything I've forgotten?'

'Do you have a morning paper?'

'Sorry. I don't have them delivered. I usually read those in the library. How about the magazine instead? Will that do? I don't suppose you had a chance to read it last night.'

Misinterpreting her mother's blank expression, Jane shrugged her shoulders.

'Sorry. I can see you're still half-asleep from all those painkillers. Perhaps you can have a proper look at it going home on the train? Personally, I preferred the cream silk to the white brocade. It's a bit late for virgin white, isn't it?' With a giggle, Jane ran to answer the telephone, leaving the bedroom door ajar. 'I expect that's Rebecca,' she called.

Liar! Rosemary thought, recoiling in disgust. Why doesn't she just admit it's Stephen? How much longer was she going to be subjected to her daughter's excited shrieks of laughter during a protracted and whispered phone conversation?

'Well, she hasn't said much. So I don't really know what she's doing. OK Leave it to me . . . Only wouldn't it be better if we had the flat to ourselves?'

Humming 'I'm Getting Married In The Morning', Jane reappeared in the doorway and adopted the familiar, wistful look she'd used so often as a child – usually when she'd been naughty or else wanted to ask for something special.

'Mum . . . you are going home today, aren't you?'

When Rosemary looked up and nodded, Jane's face was radiant. 'Oh, good! Because we're going to see Jake's new play tonight and I've told Rebecca she can stay over. I don't want you to feel you're not wanted or anything – but there won't be enough room if you're still here. Besides, Stephen was convinced you'd want to go to the cottage this weekend – it's been ages since you were there. We thought you'd want to go home and pack.'

So, this was their plan, Rosemary concluded bitterly. First they want to know where I'm going to be. Then they pretend it's Rebecca who's not only on the phone but also coming to stay at the flat. They know perfectly well I can't be in two places at once. If I'm in Norfolk, I can't be in London. Which works out admirably, leaving Stephen and Jane with the flat to themselves.

As calmly as she could, Rosemary replied, 'Don't worry. I'm definitely going home today. I feel as if I can hardly breathe in London. Having just left Sarah I know for certain she won't be needing me for a while. Some bracing North Sea breezes sound like a jolly good idea. City life doesn't appear to suit me any more. Perhaps I'm getting old?'

'Not old.' Jane grinned, nodding in the direction of the

bridal magazine. 'I'd have thought the word *mature* more appropriate.'

Fighting back tears, Rosemary turned away, hoping she'd sounded convincing enough. All she wanted to do was return home at the earliest opportunity. And although not her original intention for this weekend, she would go to the cottage after all.

Deciding to stay in bed until she heard the slamming of the front door, Rosemary removed her untouched breakfast tray to the kitchen and sighed with relief. Alone at last and finally able to enjoy some peace and quiet.

Peace and quiet. There'd been precious little of that inside the farmhouse. Not that she was complaining. She'd really enjoyed being with Sarah, Haydn and the family. Nonetheless, after the events of the past twenty-four hours, the words *peace* and *quiet* (particularly when associated with Norfolk) had a wonderfully therapeutic ring to them.

It was also a ring, in particular a somewhat loud and shrill one, which brought Rosemary back to reality. Not surprisingly, she heard Stephen's voice when she lifted the receiver.

'Rosemary. How's the head? Feeling better after a good night's sleep?'

'Mmm. Much better,' she lied, hoping to satisfy Stephen's curiosity. What was the point in telling him that every time she'd closed her eyes she'd seen him pushing the tiny ring box in Jane's direction?

'I know I said I was hoping to see you later this morning,' Stephen continued, 'but Oliver's just called and I'm going to be a bit tied up for a while longer. Are you . . . have you decided about going to the cottage?'

Concluding he already knew this and that he was merely double-checking on Jane's behalf, Rosemary reiterated her intentions. Hoping to persuade him that she'd been gullible enough to believe their plans, she announced in her brightest voice, 'Stephen, I can't thank you enough for arranging this theatre trip for Jane. I know she's been looking forward to it for ages. Why don't you come back here for a post theatre supper? Tell Jane I'll call in at M&S and get something for you before I leave.'

Returning from her shopping trip, Stephen's words, '*What a great idea. Such a pity you can't join us,*' kept repeating in her head.

With fresh salmon, new potatoes, salads, strawberries and cream, plus champagne and wine in the fridge, Rosemary laid the tiny table for two. Hunting for some candles and napkins, she was reminded of the chaos in the flat. Last night she'd been far too upset, tired and preoccupied with other matters to do anything about it.

This will have to be my final gesture, she considered sadly, moving a pile of unironed laundry. I only hope there's clean sheets in the airing cupboard. Armed with fresh linen, Rosemary began to strip the bed, spying as she did so one of Stephen's sweaters wedged between the side table and the mattress. Something else she hadn't noticed last night. Holding it close, she wrapped the empty sleeves about her, all the while trying to control the deep shuddering sobs that racked her body. The citrus and musk scent on Jane's bathrobe. It hadn't been Jane's perfume after all. It had been Stephen's cologne.

Drained of both tears and emotion and conscious of the smell of damp wool, Rosemary dabbed at the sweater with a tissue, her thoughts turning quite naturally to sheep and Wales. Reminded of Sarah's earnest voice saying, '*Just let it happen, Ro. Everything will be all right. I promise,'* Rosemary conceded defeat. 'Yes, Sarah, I will let it happen,' she murmured forlornly. 'In the circumstances it's all I can do now.'

An hour and a half later and once more in control, Rosemary made herself a coffee and hunted for pen and paper. During the past 90 minutes, channelling her energy into cleaning the flat, she'd thought hard and long about Stephen. Despite everything, she still loved him. But for his sake – and even her daughter's – she'd come to the conclusion she must at least try to be adult and civilized. Deep in her heart she already knew it wasn't going to be easy. As for putting on a brave face for whenever Jane's wedding took place . . . She frowned, her face a mixture of puzzlement and alarm. The song Jane had been humming from *My Fair Lady*. Was that supposed to be a hint? Were Jane and Stephen getting married in the morning? Had Stephen secured a special licence?

Preferring not to think in that direction, Rosemary decided her immediate task was to leave Stephen a letter. Jane could give it to him this evening, when he arrived at the flat. Keeping her words brief, saying that she thought it best if they didn't see each other for a while, she also mentioned that she was sure he'd understand and even hoped they could remain friends. In conclusion, she wished him every happiness and continued success when he returned to America to finish filming.

Before leaving the flat, she lovingly folded Stephen's sweater, left it lying on the newly made bed and placed the letter on top. As for the magazine . . . she had absolutely no desire to read that on the journey home. One look at page one hundred and nineteen had been more than enough.

Once home, hurriedly checking the house and garden to see that everything was in order, Rosemary stepped out of her smart city clothes, changed into a pair of jeans, loafers and sweatshirt, backed up the computer to the USB drive, grabbed the car keys and headed for her garage. Anything else she was likely to need would already be at the cottage.

Perhaps it was foolhardy to drive to the cottage so late on a Friday evening, she thought, stowing her laptop in the car, but the homeward train journey had taken almost twice as long as usual. Had she heard correctly? The current spate of engineering works on the line were going to last another three months, with trains stopping at Milton Keynes and passengers being transferred by coach to Watford. Another good reason for steering clear of London, Rosemary concluded. Thank goodness working from home meant she could avoid the daily commute. In fact, with things as they were at present, there was no reason at all why she couldn't de-camp to the cottage for several months.

Forcing herself to go the first hundred miles without stopping, she eventually pulled into a roadside restaurant complex for a coffee. To her dismay she discovered they were already in the process of closing, pulling down shutters and switching off lights.

'*Switching off lights*', a tiny voice murmured in Rosemary's head. She'd forgotten to warn Freda and Harry she was coming. Telling herself it was too late to ring now, she'd have to grope her way to the cottage door in darkness, Rosemary stood outside another door sporting a sign saying CLOSED.

'If you're staying at the motel you'll find a hospitality tray in your room,' a kindly voice advised.

'I'm not,' Rosemary replied, spying a young couple walking arm in arm towards the motel. For a moment she even hesitated, tempted to see if there was a vacant room. Deciding against it, she made her way back to the car.

Definitely not a good idea, she told herself, suppressing a yawn. She would prefer not to face dewy-eyed couples over breakfast in the morning.

More bleary-eyed than dewy-eyed, she picked a CD at random. At least listening to some of her favourite music, she could sing along and hopefully stay awake for the rest of the journey. Without warning, the poignant song 'Save Me' echoed almost immediately within the confines of the car, causing tears to course down her cheeks. Of all the CDs she could have chosen it had to be the one they'd played on Stephen's first visit to Romany Fields.

Poised with her finger on the OFF switch, Rosemary changed her mind. No, she had to get through this somehow. What better way to keep herself mentally alert, singing along with the hauntingly beautiful lyrics, telling of lost love and tarnished dreams.

With almost every line of every song evoking the love she felt for Stephen, Rosemary had no recollection of arriving at the cottage. Perhaps in answer to the words of the first song she'd been singing, someone had saved her after all?

Exhausted from her journey, Rosemary slept a dreamless sleep. The following morning, however, her waking thoughts weren't quite so trouble-free. Briefly trailing her fingers across the empty space beside her, it was impossible not to recall the precious moments she'd spent here with Stephen, their bodies joined together as one.

'Joined together as one,' she intoned ecclesiastically, dragging herself from the bed in the direction of the shower. From now on she must accept it would be her daughter locked in Stephen's arms, Jane who would feel Stephen's lips on her throat as he kissed and caressed her.

'Stop it. Stop it at once!' she cried, drying herself fiercely with the towel. 'For God's sake, pull yourself together. It's over, Rosemary. You have to get on with your own life. To begin with that means . . . food,' she announced with a sardonic smile. The gnawing pains and grumbling in her stomach were a reminder she'd not eaten for twenty-four hours. No wonder she'd been thinking and behaving so irrationally. Faced with bare shelves and an empty fridge, she set off for the village shop.

An hour later, sitting on a stool in the kitchen, considerably refreshed and revived, Rosemary switched on her laptop and reached for a cup of strong black coffee. Now was as good a time as any to prepare the proper copy of her typescript, concentrate on the cover blurb and even revamp her author bio. Her life had certainly changed during the past three years.

'Work – Coffee – Work – Lunch – Work – Tea – WALK!!!' instructed her hastily scribbled timetable with the words 'DO NOT GET SIDETRACKED' underlined in red felt tip.

Her first reaction when the phone rang was to ignore it. Later as the ringing became more persistent, it wasn't so easy. It could be Harry or Freda, she supposed (now they were aware of her presence) then again it could also be Jane, fresh from her lover's embrace. Had Stephen given Jane the engagement ring last night or had he waited until this morning?

'Mum!' Jane's voice called frantically. 'Where were you? You've been ages answering the phone.'

'Sorry, darling. I was in the garden,' she lied. 'Is everything OK?'

'Oh, yes. *Absolutely fantastic.* You'll never guess—'

Here it comes, Rosemary thought miserably, waiting for the avalanche of words to come snowballing down the line.

'We had such an amazing evening and the play was superb. Then Jake met us after the performance – and oh, talk about dishy and tasty. Which reminds me thanks for supper. You really went over the top there, didn't you? Rebecca said it was such a shame Jake and Stephen couldn't share it with us.'

'Rebecca? But I thought—'

'Mum. I told you Becks was staying here last night. Surely you remember? That's why I had to push you out. Although I did feel pretty awful about it afterwards. Especially with you looking so ghastly. You know what they say? Two's a party, three's a crowd, particularly in this flat.'

At that moment another excited voice echoed down the line. 'Hi, Mrs F. Thanks for the super eats and champagne. Certainly makes a change from my beans on toast and Jane's carbonara. To be honest I think we're still a bit squiffy. Either that or I'm still reeling from the thrill of meeting Stephen. Isn't he lovely? Not at all how I imagined. Gosh! Aren't you lucky?'

With Rosemary considering the word 'lucky', hardly a word she would have chosen in the circumstances, Jane came back on the line.

'Hi, Mum. Me again. Sorry about that. Rebecca hasn't stopped talking since she met Stephen. It was as much as I could do to stop her dragging him into the flat when he brought us home. Of course, I told her he was already spoken for. Don't worry, we weren't totally selfish. We did offer to share our supper with him but he declined. Poor love. He looked all in.

Thanks to Oliver who'd kept them at it until quite late.'

'Kept who at it?' Rosemary asked lamely.

'Stephen and the others, of course.'

'The others?'

'The entire cast of *To Love the Hero*. Thank goodness it was only the dubbing tapes destroyed in that horrendous fire and not the actual film.'

Pausing briefly for an intake of breath, Jane sensed her mother's bewilderment. 'You did know about the fire, didn't you? It was in all the papers. I thought Stephen had told you. Then again,' she giggled, 'I expect he's had more important things on his mind just lately. Oh, yes, while I remember, You'll be pleased to know I gave him your letter.'

The letter! Rosemary's mind was in turmoil, like a fruit machine in a seaside arcade, newly fed with coins, and Jane had just pulled the handle. Only in her case it wasn't fruit and bells that were whirling in all directions, it was people. Jane and Rebecca, Oliver and Jake, the cast of *To Love the Hero* and . . . Stephen.

'You gave Stephen my letter,' she repeated numbly.

'Of course I did. Isn't that what you wanted? I assumed it was your reply to Stephen's marriage proposal. Mind you, having spent weeks helping him plan all this, I was a bit miffed when he wouldn't tell me what you'd written. So are you going to put me out of my misery?'

Misery. Jane had never spoken a truer word. Rosemary clutched at the phone unable to move or speak.

'Mum, why aren't you saying anything? From your silence does that mean. . . you refused him? But why?' Jane cried, aghast. 'When he loves you so much and. . .'

'I didn't refuse him – because he never asked,' Rosemary struggled.

'Didn't ask? When we had lunch in The Orchard Bowl and Stephen showed me your ring, he told me—'

'*My ring*? I thought Stephen had bought it for you. I saw the photo of you both in the magazine; saw you together in the restaurant. Stephen had a ring box and he—'

There was a pregnant pause while Jane assessed the implication of what her mother was saying. How she wished she and Rebecca hadn't drunk so much last night. Her early euphoria had now given way to sheer panic, utter disbelief and the first flush of anger.

'Let's get this straight... You thought Stephen and I... That we'd actually... No! You can't have. That's preposterous. I'll admit he's a rather gorgeous prospect as a step-father and Ben also thinks he's great, but Stephen's far too old for me. Besides it's you he loves. You he wants to take back to America. That's why I suggested he had a word with Gran and Grandad about keeping an eye on Ben while...'

Sinking heavily into a chair, Rosemary heard Jane's irate voice calling down the phone. 'I still don't believe you could be so dense. Unless of course you've been spending too much time talking to all those bloody sheep! No wonder you're woolly-headed. That ring was for you, Mum. OK, so I'll admit to playing up for the paparazzi, that day outside the jewellers. I was only there because Stephen asked for my advice. He had to; he needed to know your ring size and your taste in jewellery.'

Not knowing quite how to reply, Rosemary remembered the magazine. 'Then why the *Brides* magazine?'

'Why the magazine?' Jane snorted, her expression of disgust almost risible. 'Wasn't that obvious? Or have you been away so long that you've also forgotten how to read?'

Mildly indignant, Rosemary replied, 'Of course I haven't.

That feature on page a hundred and nineteen was all about the bride's mother.'

'Oh, Jesus!' Jane sighed. 'I can't believe I said a hundred and nineteen? I thought I'd said a hundred and ninety.'

'Well, you always speak so quickly and I . . .'

'OK. Point taken. Perhaps I do and perhaps the page you looked at was the wrong one. Now will you *please* go and look at page ONE-NINE-ZERO.'

'I can't. I left the magazine behind at the flat,' Rosemary said, feeling distinctly pathetic as Jane's exasperated reply coincided with the ringing of the doorbell at the flat and Rebecca's excited squealing in the background.

'Look, Mum, I feel really awful about all this but I must go. Jake's just arrived. He's taking Becks and me for a spin in his Porsche cos they don't need him for today's matinée. He's already been to Fortnums for a picnic hamper and I thought we could take the remains of the wine from last night. We'll drink a toast to you while we're lounging by the banks of the Thames. I'm sure Jake mentioned going to Henley or Marlow. In the meantime, why don't you try and get hold of Stephen?'

Jane heard her mother's softly whispered, 'I couldn't possibly. He won't want anything to do with me now,' and then the line went dead.

In a daze Rosemary left the cottage, Jane's parting words ringing in her head. '*We'll drink a toast to you.*'

A toast for what? she thought cynically. For being the most stupid woman alive? What Ben and his peers would probably call a dork.

Without knowing where she was going, Rosemary walked aimlessly to the end of the garden, through the wicket gate and across swathes of dune grass until she reached the water's edge, all the while thinking of the wonderful times she and Stephen had shared in this delightful spot. Although the very first weekend they had spent here, when they'd become lovers, was the most special, they had also managed to snatch the odd Friday or Saturday night at the cottage when Stephen wasn't needed at the studio. Then it wasn't only the fun and laughter they shared but also tender, quiet moments spent walking barefoot in the moonlight, baring their innermost thoughts.

'It was so good. So very good,' she whispered, her voice barely audible above the crashing of the waves against the shoreline. 'Is that why I didn't expect it to last?'

According to Jane it could have lasted; it was also what Stephen had hoped for. Now all she had left were empty memories.

Halting at the water's edge, Rosemary stooped to pick up a tear-shaped pebble. Smooth and opaque she held it against her cheek where traces of sand and salt mingled with her own fresh tears. With a sudden cry of despair she flung it into the foam. 'I don't want it to end like this. Please God, let there be some other way.'

In concentrated silence she watched the tide curl round the pebble and toss it back in her direction. Perhaps it's an omen, she thought, desperate for any sign that her prayer had been answered.

With the pebble once more tantalizingly within her grasp, Rosemary waded into the waves to retrieve it. How wonderful the sea felt swirling about her ankles. In fact it was just like words from the song: 'Wash me clean . . .'

With the words of yet another song by her favourite Canadian singer whispering in her head, Rosemary sat down in the surf and marvelled at her surroundings. What could be more perfect than to be washed clean in such an idyllic setting? Tiny waves brushed against her jean-clad thighs like welcoming fingers, skylarks serenaded overhead, a gentle breeze rustled in greeting through the dune grass and golden sunlight caressed her cheeks. Could anyone ask for more?

'Of course not,' she whispered, spying a white billowy cloud that seemed strangely reminiscent of Stephen's white rose. 'Unless ... like Sleeping Beauty ... I can sleep for a hundred years?'

So saying, Rosemary clasped the tear-shaped pebble to her breast, closed her eyes and lay down in the water.

Chapter 15

'Jake. You've simply got to take me. Please!' Jane begged. 'It's an emergency. I have to speak to Stephen because I know Mum won't.'

Reluctantly succumbing to Jane's request, Jake switched on the ignition and waited for the familiar throaty roar of the engine. 'OK. I'll take you – but I have to warn you if they're recording, they won't let you in.'

'That's a risk I'm prepared to take,' Jane said, feeling sick in the pit of her stomach. If only she hadn't been quite so hasty to condemn her mother. If only she'd recognized the warning signs that day in the restaurant. The last time she'd seen her mother looking so ill was shortly after her father's funeral.

Then, three years ago, Jane had been about to embark on a university education. Probably not the best of times to appreciate and understand what her mother had been going through. It was only in recent years she'd become aware of the subsequent problems Rosemary had been left to deal with. Not only being widowed so young but also having to deal with the aftermath of Gary's ill-timed decision to remortgage their house, coupled with the financial burden of sending both her son and daughter to university.

Toying with the bulky brown envelope on her lap, Jane was consumed with guilt. She'd behaved abominably when her mother had first announced her intention to sell the large family house (complete with landscaped gardens, orchards and tennis court) and buy a brand new and much smaller property on a modern development.

'It will be like moving to a rabbit hutch,' Jane had protested.

'Albeit a rather nice rabbit hutch,' her grandad had announced on the day they'd all visited the show home together. 'At least you and Ben will still have your own bedrooms *and* there'll be a guest room for when Gran and I come to stay.'

Scowling, Jane had retorted with, 'You and Gran couldn't possibly fit in that poky little box room. It's not even big enough for a study.'

Glad to see Jake pulling into the area leading to the studio, Jane was also reminded that when Gran and Grandad had eventually come to stay, she wasn't there anyway. She was away, thoroughly enjoying her first term at university. As for her poor mother, suffering with those interminable migraines, she'd been sent to Wales to stay with Sarah, leaving Ben in the capable hands of his grandparents.

Warmed by the memory of her first Christmas vacation, when she'd returned home to find Ben helping Grandad turn that same poky little box room into a bespoke study-cum-guestroom, Jane reached for her handkerchief and blew her nose hard. In many ways that little room had probably saved her mother's sanity. How strange that once she'd started writing, all Mum's wretched migraines had simply disappeared.

'Until now,' Jane said under her breath, telling herself it was hardly surprising they'd returned with a vengeance. So far it had been one hell of a year for her mother.

Coping with her husband's infidelity, looking after Sarah, Haydn and the farm, dealing with Oliver, attempting to write another book, while all the time supporting her two children (morally and financially) and being on standby for when Gran went into hospital for her hip operation. Wasn't that enough to give anyone a headache?

Filled with a new-found pride in all her mother's achievements, Jane's thoughts turned to Stephen. He couldn't be held responsible for this current dilemma, could he? Far from giving Rosemary a headache, he had in fact brought her back to life. It was almost as if she'd been one of those rare desert plants that seldom flowered. Stephen's love had made her blossom and bloom.

'Poor Stephen, it's not his fault,' Jane said, turning to look at Jake when he eventually slew the car to an abrupt halt in the studio car park. 'It's me who's the biggest headache of all.'

Ignoring Jake's questioning gaze, Jane leapt from the car, edged her way past a burly security guard, paused to question a bewildered receptionist and ran down the dimly lit corridor. Narrowly escaping the arms of yet another guard, who tried unsuccessfully to bar her way, she spied a red NO ENTRY light and hurried towards it.

'Hey, miss. Stop! You can't go in there.'

'I must. It's a matter of life or death.'

Familiar with girls of all ages using any number of excuses to gain access to the studios and their idols (and also knowing his job could be on the line), the guard attempted a record-breaking sprint, arriving just in time to place a restraining arm across the door jamb. Jane struggled against him and made a grab for the door handle. Harsh voices emitted from inside.

'Jeez! What the hell is going on?' Oliver demanded, furious, pushing his way into the corridor.

'Stephen. I must speak to Stephen! I think Mum might have . . .' Jane cried, gasping for breath.

Oliver scowled. Somehow or other he seemed to recognize this wild-eyed young woman. Where had he seen her before?

'OK, buddy,' he said to the guard who was still grappling with Jane. 'Just hold it a minute, will you?'

Turning back to the occupants of the studio, Oliver called out. 'Take five, everyone. Seems like we have some hysterical female for you, Stephen. As you look so goddamned awful and you sure as hell ain't concentrating, we might just as well call a halt to recording.'

Relieved to be set free, Jane rubbed at her arms and looked towards the studio door. Stephen appeared through a crowd of murmuring of voices.

'Gosh! Oliver's right. You really do look awful.'

'Thanks. So would you if you hadn't slept a wink all night and—'

Not giving him a chance to continue, Jane began in her usual torrid stream. 'Stephen. If it's about Mum's letter?'

'Oh, yes. It's about her letter, all right,' he announced bitterly.

'Well, it was all a mistake.'

'Too right it was. I should never have expected . . .'

Jane reached up in a desperate attempt to grab Stephen by the shoulders. 'No! You've got it all wrong! Will you *please* listen to me?'

With scant regard to the gathering audience, Jane blurted out, 'Mum thought you and I . . . She saw the picture in that stupid magazine . . . saw us in the restaurant together. The ring – remember?'

'What about the ring?'

'Mum thought you were giving it to me. When she heard me on the phone to Becky she put two and two together and made five. Oh, Stephen, this is *truly* awful. Don't you see? Don't you understand what this means?'

No, he didn't. All he knew was that he was exhausted from pacing the floor half the night, even before he'd made a futile attempt at sleep. He'd also been deeply hurt and quite unable to understand Rosemary's coolly polite letter. 'You mean she thought. . . ? No. That's insane.'

'It is to us but look at it from Mum's perspective. The day in the restaurant when she wasn't well? I should have recognized the warning signs. Anyway, you and I both know what was supposed to happen that day. The trouble is Mum doesn't. So will you please go and tell her?'

Stephen's face broke into a slow smile. 'Jane, you're wonderful,' he cried, kissing her forehead and lifting her high into the air.

'I know, and you're far too old for me. So put me down. It's embarrassing with all these people watching.'

Scanning a sea of bewildered faces, Stephen lowered Jane carefully to the floor and fetched his jacket. 'Where is she? Is she here?'

'No. She was at the cottage,' Jane explained, her earlier smile of relief dissipating. 'But she seemed in a most dreadful state and I had such a go at her.'

Something about the underlying tone in Jane's sombre voice unnerved Stephen.

'*Was*? Jane . . . what do you mean by *was*? You don't think she could have. . . ?'

Hardly daring to think of the consequences of this awful imbroglio, Stephen closed pained, grey eyes and ran both hands through his unkempt hair. In his mind's eye he saw a map of the roads between the London studio and the cottage at Romany Fields. It would take him simply ages to get there.

'And I've hardly got any petrol and Mabel's playing up,' he muttered, rummaging in his pocket for his car keys. Utterly dejected, Stephen made eye contact with Oliver. He hardly dared ask about the sound recording.

'When you gotta go, you gotta go,' Oliver said, a twinkle in his eye as if reading his mind. 'I guess we were just about ready to wrap it up anyway.'

'And you'd better take these,' Jake called, hurrying towards him with Rebecca close behind. He tossed Stephen a bunch of car keys. 'You take mine and give me yours. Don't worry, I'll see to Mabel.'

Stephen was already running for the exit when Jane called after him. 'Stephen, wait. I almost forgot. If you find her . . . I mean when you find her, will you please give her this?' Thrusting a large crumpled envelope into his hand, Jane whispered something in his ear.

Watching him go, Jake dangled Mabel's keys apologetically in front of his two companions. 'Sorry, girls.' He grinned. 'Another day, perhaps?'

Satisfied that at least she'd been able to carry out her mission, Jane slumped against the wall. 'Oh, that doesn't matter. We can still have our picnic.'

Taking hold of Jane's hand, Jake said kindly, 'I'm afraid we can't. Haven't you forgotten something? The picnic was in the Porsche.'

Adjusting the driver's seat, Stephen stirred the bright red Porsche into life, hoping desperately Rosemary would still be at Romany Fields. Driving at speeds he hardly thought possible, he manoeuvred the car through busy London streets and the surrounding suburbs. Only when he was on the open road did he feel reassuringly in his pocket for the small box he'd been carrying for the past three days. It was there with Rosemary's letter.

With one hand on the wheel, Stephen screwed the letter into a ball and threw it on the floor in disgust. It was hard not to relive the pain and anguish of the early hours when he'd read its contents over and over again. Thank God it had all been a dreadful mistake. At least Jane had explained – albeit erratically. Even now the catalogue of confusion still filled him with alarm.

Determined to keep a clear head, Stephen remembered Oliver's party. The night when everything had spiralled hopelessly out of control. At the time his initial reaction had been one of threefold anger: his fury with Oliver for not keeping quiet about the American contract, exasperation with Rosemary because she wouldn't even discuss it with him, and more importantly, utter disgust with himself for not having enough faith in their love to ask her to marry him.

I suppose I mustn't be too hard on you, Oliver, Stephen acknowledged, convinced he was now on the last stretch of open road before the cottage. It was you who brought us together in the first place. I only hope I'm not . . . Preferring to blank out the words *too late*, Stephen drove like a man possessed. Finally, with the sound of tyres crunching on gravel, he drew the car to an abrupt halt and hurried to the front door.

Knocking and getting no reply, Stephen waited impatiently. If Rosemary wasn't inside the cottage, then she couldn't have gone far. Her car was still in the drive; even the keys were in the ignition. The keys! Stephen brightened, rubbing a hand across his unshaven chin. The spare key for Romany Fields. Taking it from the familiar hiding place, he slipped it in the lock.

Once inside the coolness of the cottage, Stephen examined the orderly remains of lunch and recent evidence of Rosemary's work. All neatly laid in chapters, they filled him with renewed hope. Rosemary was such a level-headed person. She wouldn't do anything foolish – would she? Jane was simply overreacting.

Reminded once more of Rosemary's car keys (left uncharacteristically in the car), Stephen began to feel distinctly uneasy. The cottage was too silent, too still and it unnerved him. In trepidation he made his way up the stairs, letting out a deep sigh of relief when he found both bedrooms empty.

A lump rose in his throat. Neatly folded on the bed was Rosemary's winceyette nightdress. A vivid reminder of that first wonderful night together. He sat on the edge of the bed and caressed the soft folds of fabric. 'Oh, my love. Where are you? Why aren't you here?'

His gaze darting restlessly about the room, Stephen noticed an upturned book beneath the washstand. Recognizing it to be the one Ben had bought his mother for her birthday, Stephen bent down to pick it up. Rosemary loved books. She'd never knowingly leave them on the floor.

'What the. . . ? Bloody press! Why can't you leave people alone?' he yelled, his eyes alighting on the incriminating magazine photo Rosemary had been using as a bookmark.

Anxious to destroy all evidence of that stupid photo, taken outside the London jewellers, he was about to wrench it from between the pages of the book when conscience got the better of him. There must be something else he could use as a bookmark.

Reaching into his wallet, Stephen found the stub from his recent boarding card. Certainly not the best thing to choose, since it only served to remind him that very soon he must return to the States, but a darned sight better than that wretched magazine cutting. Carefully placing the book on the bed by Rosemary's nightdress, he moved towards the open window.

For several minutes Stephen stood staring out, his eyes scanning the distant dunes and seashore. All to no avail. Everywhere was calm and still until a sudden unexpected gust of offshore breeze stirred the tussocky grasses into life. Only then did he discern the minutest splash of colour amongst the pale green and yellow of the dune bank.

Hope surged through Stephen's breast. It could be Rosemary . . . Then again it could also be a courting couple, wanting to be left in peace. He would have to be very discreet.

From her secluded spot amongst the marram grass, Rosemary lay with closed eyes, basking in the late afternoon sunshine. Her tears and clothes had long since dried and she found the gentle heat radiating from the warmth of the sand beneath her strangely comforting. Only once had the enveloping stillness been broken by the roaring engine of a high-performance car.

'Maniac,' she'd whispered lazily, glimpsing a flash of red on the distant, black ribbon that was the road.

Resenting the intrusion into her becalmed state of mind, she contemplated going back to the cottage and her manuscript. The only problem being that returning to Romany Fields and the approaching night also meant returning to fresh memories of Stephen. It was impossible not to think of him. Losing him would be like losing part of herself. Now all she had left was nothing but empty dreams and a living hell. To think that only a few short weeks ago she'd even been foolish enough to liken their relationship to that of the hero and heroine in her latest novel, joined together as one.

'How very ironic,' Rosemary acknowledged with a whisper. Also joined together as one were two cinnabar moths flying overhead. Shielding her eyes against the dazzling sunlight, she watched them dipping and darting above a clump of yellow ragwort, their delicate wings seemingly coupled together by an invisible thread.

With her fascinated gaze taking in their distinctive black and red stripes and two red spots, she was immediately transported back to Bramhall Lane football ground. She gave a wan smile, reminded of the time she'd walked along this stretch of beach with Stephen, not only teasing him about the black and yellow caterpillars, but also explaining how one day they would metamorphose into Sheffield United supporters.

Scarlet and black. Everything was scarlet and black, she concluded. Sheffield United's football strip, the black T-shirt she was wearing decorated with bright scarlet poppies, the distinctive coloured cinnabar moths and even the speeding sports car, flashing by on shiny black tarmac.

What was it the experts said about scarlet and black? Warning colours. It was certainly true of the cinnabar. The red hind wings with black edges were a definitive warning to predators of their bitterly unpleasant taste.

It was a warning of a different kind that caused Rosemary to start in alarm. The instantly recognizable crunch of footsteps on the shingle path beyond the dunes told her that she was no longer alone. Please. No day-trippers, she begged. Not today of all days.

Anxiously awaiting the sound of approaching voices, Rosemary eased herself on to her stomach and waited. To her surprise there were none. She blinked against the sunlight. Perhaps she'd just imagined intruders . . . but no, there it was again. The rasp-like sound of footsteps. Only this time on sand. This time getting nearer.

Rosemary froze, conscious of her heart pounding in her breast and blood coursing through her veins. Like a cornered animal she must keep perfectly still and wait for the danger to pass. Still craving solitude, no one must know that she was here.

Without warning, gentle hands gripped her shoulders and raised her carefully to her feet. 'Stephen!' she gasped, falling into his arms. 'Stephen . . . the letter . . . I'm so sorry. It was all a terrible mistake.'

'Shh. It's all right, my darling,' he soothed, stroking her hair. 'There's no need for tears. Jane has explained everything.'

'But I thought I'd lost you.'

'No.' Stephen smiled, brushing dried grains of sand and tears from her cheeks. 'You've not lost me but I've found you, even though it took an awful long time to fathom out where you were.'

Returning arm in arm to the cottage Stephen handed her the bulky, dog-eared brown envelope. 'By the way, Jane says I'm to give you this with the cryptic message *one hundred and ninety*. Does that make any sense to you?'

Swallowing back tears, Rosemary removed the copy of *Brides* magazine and began turning the pages as instructed.

'I don't quite know how to take that,' she said, reaching for her handkerchief. 'I didn't think I was that old.'

Stephen grinned, peering over her shoulder at the feature

headline: 'Dresses For The Mature Bride'. 'You're not, but if you are going to be a bride, can I suggest you begin by taking this? I only hope you like it.'

Removing the tiny box from his pocket, Stephen took the single solitaire with its unusual setting, and placed it on her finger. 'It's Victorian – so also slightly mature,' he teased. 'But a certain someone told me you're not too keen on modern jewellery. And, because you've got such small fingers, I also had to have it altered.'

'I know. Jane told me. Can you ever forgive me for being so stupid?'

Stephen nodded and lifted her fingers to his lips. 'Let's talk about that later, shall we? Right now all I want to do is make love to you. Do you realize how much time we've wasted through our own foolishness?'

Not waiting for a reply, he promptly lifted her into his arms and, ignoring her protests to put her down, edged his way up the narrow staircase.

Sated and safe in his embrace, Rosemary whispered, 'If only I'd behaved more rationally when Oliver broke the news of your American contract.'

'Hmm. I'm afraid I did let rip at him about that. What with the fire at the studio, he's also had rather a rough time of it just lately. At least it was only the dubbing tapes, not the reels of film that were destroyed.'

'Do you know, I never even knew anything about it. When I was in Wales I never had time to read the papers.'

'No, only magazines,' Stephen said with a laconic smile.

Knowing precisely which magazine Stephen was referring to, Rosemary explained. 'I didn't read that in Wales, I saw it at Euston, just before I met you and Jane for lunch.'

'Then no wonder you thought...' Stephen began, reminded of the catalogue of horrors that had threatened to destroy their happiness. 'Jane only told me half the story. As for poor Oliver. If only you could have seen his face. Still, I suppose we should be grateful that he did feel guilty about us. I don't think he would have let me leave otherwise.'

Describing the commotion in the studio and Jane's rather public outburst, Stephen continued, 'You should have seen your daughter's performance. It was brilliant.'

'I still can't believe she was capable of doing that.'

'Oh, I can assure you she was. At the time Oliver wasn't the only one who was furious. However, once she explained what had happened I didn't give a damn what Oliver thought. Or anyone else for that matter.'

'And Jake the hero came to the rescue,' Rosemary mimicked in a soft American drawl.

'Sure did, ma'am. In fact, it was just like the movies. Perhaps you should write a book about it.'

'Perhaps I should,' Rosemary said, her eyes filling with sadness.

'Rosemary? What's wrong?'

'It's hearing you talk of *movies* and knowing that you have to return to the States.'

'Yes. I do. But this time will be different. This time I want you to come back with me. It's not as if I'm asking you to leave your family for good.'

'Only if it's what you really want?'

'What I really want? I'm surprised you even have to ask. Don't you realize that you are all that I want. All I've ever wanted, in fact – from the moment I first gave you that white rose. I swear I'm never going to lose you again.'

With no further doubts in their minds the only problem

was making all the arrangements. There was so much to think of. Despite Rosemary's concerns, Stephen already knew Ben and Jane wouldn't be a problem. Jane had made sure of that first by contacting her grandparents and then contacting Ben himself, who after a first year in halls was already planning to move into a rented house with three other students. As for Jane, thanks to Jake, there was even a strong possibility that she had found herself a job in London.

'Don't look so worried,' Stephen said, picking up the phone to ring Oliver. 'While Ben's in Sheffield I'll make sure my sisters keep an eye on him. Mary's a brilliant cook and my nephews are mad keen on football, ice-skating and cricket. As I mentioned before, we shan't be away for ever. You'll still be able to send him your own version of Red Cross food parcels.'

Rosemary held up her hands in mock surrender. 'OK, I give in but I still can't believe how all this plotting went on behind my back. Anyway . . . tell me, how was Oliver?'

'First, he says I've got to give you a big hug and a kiss and second, he says to tell you he's no longer tearing his hair out. Which is quite a relief, really, he's so precious little of it left.'

'Not like you,' Rosemary said, fixing Stephen with a loving smile, while stroking the hair that fell heavily across his forehead.

'And to think I still haven't combed my hair or had a shave,' Stephen replied, rubbing at the stubble on his chin. 'Do you know your daughter actually told me I looked awful?'

'Then she's wrong. I think you look lovely.'

'Nevertheless, I still think I should go and tidy myself up.'

Finding him some toiletries and a clean towel, Rosemary dumped them unceremoniously in his lap. 'Which reminds me, Mr Walker. In future I'd like you to refrain from wearing my daughter's bathrobe!'

'Her what?'

'Jane's bathrobe. When I was at the flat I noticed it smelt suspiciously of your aftershave.'

Stephen paused, deeply pensive. 'Ah, I see what you're getting at. Well, it would wouldn't it? Considering I had to borrow it the night I stayed there and slept on the sofa.'

'And what about your sweater, wedged beside her bed?'

'Goodness! You have been doing a Miss Marple. All I can say to that is I'm completely innocent, m'lud. Jane borrowed it one evening because she was cold. She said pure wool was a great deal warmer than what she usually wears.'

Reminded of Jane's hipster jeans and crop tops, Rosemary looked up into soft grey eyes and snorted playfully. 'Hmph. If you don't mind I'd prefer not to think of what my daughter usually wears. Perhaps the sooner we're married the better.'

'I'll certainly second that,' Stephen said, bending down to kiss Rosemary full on the mouth.

Chapter 16

Turning away from the window where she'd been admiring the impressive New York skyline, Rosemary rearranged the group of assorted family photos: Jane's graduation, Ben on a recent field trip, her parents' golden wedding, Ted standing proudly on his allotment and last of all Sarah's twin lambs. Everything had worked out perfectly. Even the baby girls – Bethany and Hanna – had timed their arrival so she could be there at the birth before flying out to join Stephen in New York.

'How are you getting on with Miriam?' Stephen called from the bathroom.

'Really well. Or should that be *swell?* Although I confess I'm still a bit wary of the party she and Oliver are throwing for us this evening.'

'Why is that?' Intrigued by the embarrassed silence, Stephen wandered into the bedroom and fixed a towel about his waist. 'Aren't you going to tell me?'

Rosemary twisted the engagement ring on her finger. 'If you really want to know . . . it's because Miriam keeps asking me when we're getting married.'

'That's not a problem, is it? What did you tell her?'

'I told her that you'd never asked me. At least not properly.'

Stephen looked on in amazement. 'Goodness! You're right. I didn't, did I? I'd intended to ask you that day at Romany Fields, when Jane sent me with the magazine. Somehow I never got round to it, though. I suppose you could say we were, er, side-tracked.'

Rosemary coloured at the memory. Jane had questioned her about the magazine article, of course, but other than reading the headline there hadn't been time for anything else.

Stephen walked towards her. 'Hmm. As the saying goes, there's no time like the present. Perhaps I should ask you now.'

'Dressed like that? You're only wearing a towel.'

'And why not? At least my intentions are honourable . . . aren't they?'

With the mischievous glint in his eyes that Rosemary had come to love and recognize, Stephen got down on one knee. 'Rosemary, will you marry me?'

Looking down at him kneeling before her, his hair and body still damp from the shower, Rosemary placed her hands on his shoulders and whispered, 'Stephen, my darling, I love you so much but . . .'

Trapped by the towel and unable to move, when the sharp ringing of the telephone cut through the air of expectancy like a knife, Stephen could only watch, helpless. Rosemary caressed his cheek with trailing fingers and hurried across to the far corner of the apartment to answer the phone.

Smiling at his predicament, Stephen hissed, 'It's probably

only Miriam checking up on us. Tell her not to worry – we will be there and we've also got some good news.'

Rosemary turned towards him, her face solemn. 'I'm afraid we haven't, Stephen. It's not Miriam, it's Mary. Your father's had an accident.'

'He's what?'

Stephen struggled to the phone, trailing the towel behind him. At any other time it would have made an amusing scenario. Not tonight, however. His face was etched with concern, not laughter, as he listened to his sister's voice.

'That bloody bike! I told him to stop using that damned thing ages ago. How bad is he? OK. I'll come right away. What? You have to be joking! There's no way I can agree to that . . . Oh, all right. But tell him I'm not happy about it and I may well change my mind.'

Listening to their conversation – or at least Stephen's side of it – Rosemary presumed Ted Walker was still alive. That in itself was reassuring but how badly was he injured? And what would happen next? Father and son were incredibly close. Unfortunately, Stephen was also in the middle of filming.

Passing Stephen his bathrobe, Rosemary motioned to their clothes all laid out neatly on the bed, ready for the party. 'I'd better put these away. I expect you'll want to start packing?'

'No.'

'No? But—'

'Dad says I'm not to go. I've got to stay here and finish the film. Can you believe he even made Mary promise to make me stay?' Sitting down on the bed, Stephen buried his head in his hands and muttered, 'He always was such an awkward old bugger.'

'Am I correct in thinking he's fallen off his bike?'

'Yes. He was on his way to the allotment. No doubt to check on the Chrysanths he grows for Mother's grave.'

Sensing Stephen's feeling of acute and utter helplessness, Rosemary sat down beside him and pulled him close. She couldn't bear to think of Ted lying injured in hospital, let alone Stephen suffering like this.

Moments later she strode purposefully to the wardrobe and took out a suitcase.

'Rosemary? What are you doing? You heard what Mary said. You also know how determined and stubborn Dad is.'

'Yes. I do. That's *why* I'm going and going now – before he realizes his mistake. Correct me if I'm wrong – your father only told you not to go. There was no mention of me.'

A slow smile crept over Stephen's face. 'You're right,' he said, registering her intention. 'Are you sure you don't mind? It goes without saying as I've only just managed to get you here, I can't bear to see you leave. The thought of saying goodbye for a second time . . .' Stephen rose from the bed and paced the floor. 'God, this is awful. On the other hand . . . I'd feel a damn sight happier if you could go and check up on him. At least you'll give me an honest report on his progress. Not tell me what the old devil wants me to hear.'

At JFK airport Stephen held Rosemary close, hardly daring to let her go.

'Promise me you'll ring the moment you arrive,' he said huskily.

'I promise. I'll also go straight to the hospital, regardless of time. They're bound to let me see him when they know I've flown in from the States. I shall miss you terribly,' she whispered, choking back a sob.

*

Ted's face was ghostly pale as he lay with eyes closed against crisply laundered sheets. Yes, he was still very much an older version of the man she loved so desperately, but his cheeks were gaunt and hollow and his breath barely audible. For one truly awful moment, she thought that he wasn't even breathing.

Looking up, Rosemary felt a reassuring hand upon her arm.

'Don't worry,' a sympathetic voice announced, 'he is going to be all right. It's going to take a bit of time, that's all. Although his hip is badly broken, I can assure you he'll look much better once he's recovered from the anaesthetic.'

'Has he said anything? Does he need anything?'

'Not really,' the nurse replied. 'Other than to give strict instructions not to worry Stephen and not to forget his Chrysanthemums.'

'That figures,' Rosemary said, relieved.

Yawning and overcome by tiredness, she thanked the nurse for the chair, sat down to wait and felt her eyelids beginning to droop. An hour later, when she opened them, she saw Ted's eyes gazing incredulously into hers.

'Rosemary, lass! What are you doing here?'

'Hello, Ted. Isn't it obvious? I've come to look after your Chrysanthemums.'

Ted's face filled with pain as he struggled to sit up. 'Stephen's not here, is he? I told him *not* to come!'

Rosemary put out a restraining hand. 'No. He's not here but he sends his love. So you're to promise to lie back, follow doctors' orders and get better as soon as you can.'

Without Stephen, the days and weeks that rolled into one

left her so bereft and empty, yet she only had to look at Ted to see the family likeness. At times it was almost unbearable. Eventually, deciding to make better use of her time, she turned her attention to the allotment. There was already so much to do.

Mentally prepared for the attack, armed with a pair of wellingtons and the keys to Ted's potting shed, Rosemary came to the conclusion flowers and weeds were exactly like relationships. The loving ones took time to develop, just like precious blooms, whereas arguments and misunderstandings sprung up (almost overnight and without warning) like weeds.

With trepidation she continued where Ted had left off with the Chrysanthemums. First pinching out side shoots, in order to produce finer blooms, then getting to grips with the ever-present pests, earwigs. As far as the rest of the allotment was concerned, that was far beyond her capabilities. What it needed now was manpower and lots of it. How on earth had Ted managed to cope for so long all on his own?

Fired with renewed inspiration, Rosemary enlisted the help of Ben and his fellow housemates and struck up a bargain. Some of her home cooking and baking in exchange for some heavy labour. What could be a more perfect solution?

As Ted began showing signs of improvement, he also became exceedingly fractious and impatient. Chancing upon a solitary clump of ragwort near a neighbouring allotment, Rosemary came up with an idea. An idea that reminded her of happier times spent with Stephen at the cottage.

Such carefree days, she recalled, when they'd walked hand

in hand along the seashore listening to the industrious buzz of insects and skylarks singing on the wing. At least there the idyllic peace hadn't been shattered by the distorted scratching of four personal stereos, each playing a different tune. (That's if you could call them tunes.) Reaching for a pair of secateurs, Rosemary plucked a tiny sprig of ragwort and twenty minutes later, carrying an armful of Ted's finest Chrysanthemums, headed in the direction of Meadowhall shopping centre and eventually the hospital.

It was there a bemused Mary and family found Ted sitting up in bed, wired for sound and conducting an imaginary orchestra. He was also surrounded by magnificent blooms of russet, ochre, ruby and gold.

'Aye. But this is grand,' Ted said, removing the earphones as the strains of Ivor Novello faded away. Studying both his visitors and his flowers he announced, 'Hasn't the lass done a grand job? Y'know, I couldn't have done it better misself.'

Patting the side of the bed, Ted moved his portable CD player to safety and motioned for Rosemary to sit.

'C'mon, lass. Sit yerself down because I want to ask you a question.'

Convinced Ted was going to ask about the rest of the produce on his allotment, Rosemary couldn't believe her ears when his voice reverberated across the ward. 'Now then, what I want to know is, when are you going to marry my lad?'

Taken completely unawares, and blushing as deep as the ruby-red Chrysanthemums, Rosemary felt all eyes of the family, fellow patients, staff and visitors turn in her direction.

'Well, I – um— Actually . . .'

'*Actually*, what Rosemary is really trying to say,' said a distinctly familiar voice, 'is that I just happened to be in the process of asking her to marry me when I was informed that a certain awkward someone had fallen off his bike.'

'Stephen! How?' Rosemary began, her eyes wide with astonishment. 'I mean when did you. . . ? I only spoke to you yesterday. You never said.'

'I know,' he replied, grinning wickedly and taking her in his arms. 'Because I didn't know myself until the very last minute. Business class ticket on a jumbo jet, courtesy of Miriam and Oliver, by way of an early wedding present – I hope. And . . .' He delved into his pocket and produced a familiar bunch of car keys.

'Porsche – courtesy of Jake,' she finished for him, tears threatening to spill over, while she watched him turn to embrace his father.

Ted fumbled in his pyjama pocket for a blue and white checked handkerchief and blew his nose noisily. 'I don't know, lad. Some people have all the luck.'

'Perhaps they think I deserve it,' Stephen said thoughtfully, turning back to look at Rosemary. 'Well. . . ?'

'Well, what?'

'Don't you think I deserve an answer to my question? I've come one hell of a long way for your reply. Of course I realize I'm not dressed in exactly the same way but the question remains the same. Rosemary Fielding, will you marry me?'

Rosemary's fingers played nervously with the small sprig of ragwort pinned on to her jacket. In no way could the tiny yellow flowers be compared to the magnificent blooms Ted Walker grew for his wife, yet the memories they provoked were just as precious. Blinking back tears, she looked up into Stephen's face. The cinnabar moths they'd seen in Norfolk had had their summer. Now it was autumn and their time had passed. Unlike the cinnabar she and Stephen had their whole future together.

'Yes,' she whispered, her face radiant. 'The answer is yes.'

Loud cheers drowned out Stephen's sigh of relief as he enfolded her in his arms and bent to kiss her.

'Phew! Thank heavens for that,' Ted's voice boomed across the ward. 'Now perhaps I can have a nice cup of tea.'